SALVAGED

DROWNED EARTH

DROWNED EARTH

Eight novellas.
Eight Australian authors.
One watery apocalypse.

Scientists said that it would take 5000 years for Earth's
oceans to rise.

They were wrong.

After an asteroid collides with Antarctica, a tsunami
devastates the world's coastal cities and escalates the melting
of the ice caps.

These eight novellas set in various locations around Australia
explore the potential consequences of such a catastrophe.
They can be read in any order.

Prequel short story: Shards of Silver by Alanah Andrews
The Rise by Sue-Ellen Pashley
Fire Over Troubled Water by Nick Marone
Submerged City by Austin P. Sheehan
Tides of War by Marcus Turner
The Jindabyne Secret by Jo Hart
River of Diamonds by S. M. Isaac
Emoto's Promise by Shel Calopa
Salvaged by C.A. Clark

SALVAGED

C. A. CLARK

DROWNED EARTH

First published by Deadset Press in 2020

www.aussiespeculativefiction.com

ISBN: 978-0-6487973-1-9

Cover design Copyright © Alanah Andrews

Edited by Alanah Andrews & Austin P Sheehan

www.aussiespeculativefiction.com

DEDICATION

Dedicated to my friends and family, who believe in me when I don't.

PROLOGUE

New Melbourne: a far-from-glittering jewel. A hard-won utopia of academics and scientists earnestly trying to bring technology and education back to a broken world.

Built around the remains of the high-rise buildings in the CBD, the floating city is anchored to the submerged inner-city suburbs. Thirty kilometres from the mainland shores to the east, west and north, it is held solidly in the arms of a perimeter wall which every citizen is taught to patrol and defend from the day they turn fifteen.

The wall runs from the submerged base of the Westgate Bridge, along the Yarra Flow, to what was once Federation Square. It cuts north through Collingwood and the old Melbourne Museum, then across to where the zoo once housed the last beautiful specimens of lost animal species. It forms a V point at the edge of North Melbourne where the marina has developed, before running across to Footscray, then back down to the bridge.

Sixty years since the catastrophic event, New Melbourne is emerging as the epicentre of knowledge, training and hope for recovering the best of what was lost in the Rise.

CHAPTER ONE

A light predawn breeze rippled the silver surface of the quiescent ocean. A lone jogger navigated the perimeter path in the dull grey light, warm breath-clouds disappearing in her wake.

She stopped and rested her hands on her knees, catching her breath and letting her heart rate drop. She turned her head slowly to look through her hair in both directions for any of the duty guards. As soon as she was sure she was alone, she reached for the cracks in the top of the breakwater wall, part-jumped and part-scrambled up, swinging her legs over and carefully negotiating the slippery outer edge, down to the exposed rooftops of the reinforced buildings below. The tide was out far enough to find a space to sit and watch the dawn emerge across the endless southern ocean in solitude.

She folded her arms across her knees and rested her chin on them. A tiny sigh puffed warm from her lips.

Unfolding a little solar and wind tripod, she hung her phone beneath it. The tiny silver blades spun slowly in the breeze. She scrolled for a radio station and slid the volume up a notch.

'. . . good morning, New Melbournites! It's another beautiful calm-before-the-storm sunrise, so shake off the sleepies . . . this is your favourite air jockey bringing you the best mix of BTR and ATR tunes . . .'

The phone flashed, but she hesitated before accepting. "Too early Vin, what's up?"

"Happy birthday, Cassie. Where are you hiding?"

Her momentary smile blew away in the breeze. "Thanks for reminding me, Vin. I don't have to tell you where I am on my day off."

'. . . a golden oldie to take us into the news . . .' Something early twenty-first century bounced from the speaker.

"I don't know why they keep playing that old crap." Cassie screwed up her nose. "I doubt even our grandparents would remember BTR."

"At least you had grandparents, Cass." Vin's voice held a well-practised reprimand. "And it has only been sixty years, so there are plenty of people who still remember before the asteroid and the Rise—some of us studied history, you know."

"I didn't have to study history with Granddad always going on and on about how we lost the MCG and the greatest game in the world and making me recite the names of all the lost suburbs and Grandnan demanding I repeat useless historical trivia ad nauseam, you know she was obsessed with—"

"Yeah, look, I hate to be the harbinger of bad news and cut off your happy family reminiscence, but there is a big one brewing. All the boats are anchored in North Melbourne marina and we're being called in to batten down the hatches. We've a huge stockpile of food in Eureka waiting to be delivered to the trade boats and it is pretty exposed, we can't affor—"

"Okay, you don't need to treat me like a kid Vin, I know when a storm is brewing as well as you do. I'll be there when I finish my breakfast." She touched the off button on her ear clip and leaned back against the concrete barrier.

'. . . from the mainland. The water raids are putting strain on the inland communities and rationing has been tightened . . .'

Why don't they desal? Cassie shrugged and bit into her seaweed roll. *Mainlanders are crazy.*

She stared out to the southern horizon across

endless water and chewed slowly. This was her favourite view. In New Melbourne, finding space to be alone was hard, but down here on these old rooftops she was guaranteed solitude.

Her phone flashed again. Cassie's shoulders dropped a little.

So much for solitude.

"What now, Vin?" A sigh punctuated her greeting.

"I forgot to ask if you want to come to Box Hill Island with us on the weekend?"

"Mmmm, maybe."

"Also, I told the boss I'm sending messages to your house comm so he thinks you're home. He said you need to move your backside or have it kicked."

"Sure. Who's doing the kicking?" She cut off Vin's laugh with the press of a button and settled back against the wall. The chill breeze off the ocean lifted the tendrils of her hair and bit her cheeks. The still beauty of the ocean belied the oncoming storm.

'In the beachside suburb of Melton, three people have been killed in a clash with Combers. One survivor is in a critical condition in Djerriwarrh hospital fighting for her life. A witness claimed they were packing up their belongings when the Combers . . .'

Savouring the last salty mouthful of seaweed roll, Cassie stood and stretched, turning to the east to watch the sun slide over the Dandenongs. The mountains stood in shadow thirty kilometres away across almost empty water, dotted with a few islands like Box Hill between the perimeter wall and the beach suburbs in the foothills. A sliver of salmon pink touched the top of the ranges, rapidly bleeding orange to vivid red. The red lingered for several minutes before the sun pushed above the tree line and the sky changed to washed-out blue.

Red sky at morning, we all take warning.

She removed her ear clips, folded the tripod away and wrapped it, with her phone, in a towel. She shoved the bundle in her backpack just in time.

"Hey you, kid!"

She jumped at the voice booming down and looked up to a face peering over the wall.

"What are you doing out there? No one outside the perimeter."

Her heart thundered in her chest. "Sorry, I'll be right up."

"What's your name?"

She didn't answer, concentrating on making her nervous fingers find the first holds on the crumbling concrete. A few calming breaths and she continued, swift and sure-footed. She was over the wall in minutes. She dropped softly to the path and smiled sweetly as she faced the barrier patrol member.

"Oh, it's you, Miss Orm." The man's voice was tinged with frustration. "I've told you a dozen times not to go out there, those old buildings could collapse any time and the tide comes in fast. The outer barrier doesn't stop that, as you well know. We don't have the people to rescue one stupid fool, even if it is *you*." He rubbed his chin with a thumb and forefinger, then pointed at her. "If I catch you out here again I will have to report you to your supervisor. Now get back to your work sector before the storm hits."

Cassie mock-saluted the man and leapt lightly onto the walkway beside the neat rows of houseboats in a residential waterway. Most of the high-rise buildings—or what was left of them—in the CBD were taken up with food production and training. With the exception of North Melbourne Marina where all the trade boats came in for business, the rest of the space was tightly packed and neatly stacked with residential houseboats or hydroponic garden barges with little canals between for movement. Despite the population restriction dictated by limited space, it seemed to Cassie like there were more residents all the time.

"Hey, Dave." She stopped to watch an older man uncouple the extractor from the last houseboat in the street. The boards bounced gently under her feet. "How did you get dunny duty again?"

"Swapped it for my perimeter duty; you know I hate it out there, it's boring and I would be useless if it ever came to an actual raid." He grunted and hefted the coupling back into its cradle on the sewage barge. Sunlight glinted off his thick glasses.

"I love it out there."

"I am sure you do, Cass. All running and dancing in the sun, but no actual work, hey?" Dave chuckled but she felt the judgement in his words.

First Vin and now Dave? Her slender shoulders lifted in a casual shrug. "It's not my fault there hasn't been an attack in over a decade, but you can swap with me anytime, okay."

"I'll hold you to that, Cass. See ya. Oh and hey, happy birthday." Dave raised his arm to wave as the barge moved slowly around the corner into the next canal.

Yeah, another happy damn birthday. It's still early, I could go home and check if they actually sent a message this year?

She turned north toward the towers at the centre of the city and ran across the outer floats toward the coracle bank not far from the green belt. Grabbing a paddle from the rack, she stepped into the nearest boat. The vast canyons between the buildings were still in shadow this early in the morning, but Cassie knew her city intimately and made her way towards the Eureka tower.

The sun sat a cap of golden light on the tops of the sky-scrapers; the plants cascading down the sides of the buildings seemed to stretch up to drink it in, the bright light and green foliage hiding the broken facades. She turned left into Spencer Channel and then right into the green belt along Yarra Flow. The seaweed glistened thick and dark just below the surface. Tangles of dark drying seaweed hung from poles attached to every building. The rising sun squeezed out the pungent aroma of the rotting pieces at the water's edge.

"Gack, it stinks." Cassie covered her mouth with the top of her shirt and kept paddling. Sweat began to trickle down her sides as she pushed through the green belt between the tallest buildings at the centre of the city. She tilted her head back and let the breeze cool some of the sweat out of her hair.

Why did I come this way? And why are we still calling it level twenty-six? It's not as if we can use any of the lower levels.

Vin stood in the gaping hole that served as entry to level twenty-six. He reached out a hand to catch the tether and pulled her onto the landing. "Hey Cass, about time you arrived."

She stowed the oar in the rack and tied up the coracle. "I took the Yarra instead of City Flow."

"Idiot." He ruffled her hair and pulled her into a

choke hold. "Come on, the boss is throwing a fit and we have a whole building to prep before the storm. Sorry about your day off."

Cassie shrugged her friend's heavy arm off her shoulders. "No biggie, I'll go diving next time, then no one can call me."

"Speaking of which, keep that phone hidden before you get us both in trouble. You'll never get phone privileges the usual way, so don't lose it."

His laugh caught like a fish hook in her stomach but, with some effort, she kept the smile on her face. Slapping his back, she sprinted ahead into the interior of the tower. "I might surprise you some day, Vin. Let's get to work."

The morning sped past, the storm rolling closer. Wind whipped any small unsecured items scuttling, past the people racing around locking shutters and strapping down crates.

"Cassie, there's a block in the toilet plumbing on level thirty-seven. Leave what you're doing and go fix it." Old Mark's voice cut easily through the howling wind.

Cassie frowned and flung her hands up in an age old gesture. "Why me? Any cadet can fix that. This is the tenth time today you've sent me to do a fifteen-year-old's job."

"Cassie, I teach fifteen year old kids all of these

tasks"—he waved his hand around the room indicating dive equipment and salvage nets—"and I know you learned them all quickly and precisely when you were fifteen. But now, as an adult, you don't want any sort of adult responsibility, so go fix the toilet like the child you wish to remain."

Cassie snorted a puff of air through her nostrils. "Here we go, another lecture about how hard-won this place was and we all need to take our rightful place and work together for the greater good; people died, blah blah blah?"

Old Mark stepped back, a world of hurt in his eyes. A hard knot of guilt formed in Cassie's abdomen; she knew Old Mark had lost loved ones in the battles.

Why can't I just shut up? Brain into gear before mouth . . . damn.

She glanced around at the others in her team. They were all working hard and looking anywhere else, but she could tell they were all listening. Hot blood flooded her cheeks.

"I don't like your attitude, girl." Old Mark pointed at her.

Cassie folded her arms tight across her chest, creating a barrier between her and Old Mark's gnarled accusing finger. With her cheek almost touching one shrugging shoulder, she worked up her best sassy attitude, complete with practised sneer and a flick of hair.

Old Mark studied the arthritic knobs of his knuckles for a moment, then let out a long sad breath, his shoulders drooping over his emptying lungs. He shook his head slowly from side to side.

"You, you have nothing to complain about, but you squander every opportunity given you to be a leader, to prove your worth. Wasting anything here is anathema to what we stand for and you are wasting all of your training. Training that your parents—"

"Right!" Cassie cut him off mid-sentence, chopping the air with the side of her hand. "It all comes back to them, doesn't it? My famous bloody parents, saviours of the planet, the idols of modern times, soaring in the glorified heights that everyone expects me to aspire to."

She paced as she spoke, slapping the back of one hand into the palm of the other and dramatising her words with agitated gestures. The sounds of water slapping the walls and the wind howling through the gaps lent a dramatic counterpoint to her rising anger.

"Shove your lecture, Old Mark because I don't care. It's ancient history and I don't care if people died before I was born, I don't care if there used to be raiders, I don't care how hard-won this place was and I sure as oncoming storms don't give a rat's rear end about what my very absent parents thought I should do. You can't fault any of my work. I do my share, I do my duties, I'm on time, I do everything I am supposed to do. Talk to me if you have a problem with my actual work." She picked up her backpack and strode away.

Old Mark reached toward her retreating back, then put his hand on Vince's shoulder. "Lad, would you go after her? See she doesn't get in any strife?"

Vince shook his head and watched as Cassie almost, but not quite, ran away. "Not when she's in that mood. No way. You probably shouldn't have mentioned her folks, especially today, with it being her birthday. She'll find a safe bolt-hole and cool off, eventually, then turn up to say sorry."

"Yes, I know." Old Mark sighed again and shook his head. "She doesn't realise the importance of her parents' work."

"Yeah, well some kids just want their parents around for special days."

"She isn't a child anymore, Vince, and she's wasting her training, potential, and her life. It's time she grew up and took some responsibility." Old Mark herded the team toward the lunch room. "All right everyone, finish up and we'll break for lunch. Looks like we eat Cassie's cake without her."

Vince stood and looked in the direction Cassie had

gone. He thought about how many birthdays her parents had missed, how many school events his parents had cheered at while hers were away replanting forests or saving some rare animal, soaking up ocean pollution or building sewerage systems. He recalled how many times she had bravely pretended it didn't matter.

"Yeah, but . . ."

. . . sometimes saving the world should take a back seat to at least one birthday cake.

"Stay safe, Cassie."

CHAPTER TWO

The wind caught Cassie on the platform, almost knocking her into the water. She swore and kept swearing as she leapt into the boat, almost capsizing it. The wind pushed at her back, making her return passage swifter than the morning slog.

In spite of the relative protection of the high buildings, the imminent storm was creating plenty of movement in the water and the wind raced through the corridors between them. She invented a few new words that would have shocked her mother as she struggled to pull the little vessel into its moorings, with the wind fighting to tug it out of her hands.

Cassie barely kept her footing on the floating walkways, slippery with the choppy waters and the rising wind pushing at her. She was soaked to the skin by the time she made it to her houseboat.

The houseboat rocked violently. The things she had neglected to tie down and stow skittered across the floor. A sudden loud clatter made her jump as a bowl rebounded from its impact with the fridge door.

And now I remember why we stay out of houseboats in storms; lucky it's plastic.

She pressed the power button on the computer and picked up the bowl, tidying a few things in a distracted manner while it booted up. Her inbox was as empty as she expected and emptier than she had hoped.

No 'happy birthday' this year either?

Cassie angrily stabbed the shutdown button and grabbed her wetsuit from the drying rack beside the door.

I'll have to go deep and quiet. Maybe I'll just stay down there.

The cold clammy material, still damp from her previous dive, proved difficult to slide on, even with her feet and ankles well lubed. Tugging and sliding, swearing and pulling, she finally rested with the thick skin rolled at mid-thigh.

I'll never get this over my rashie today. No one will notice anyway, and they wouldn't care if they did.

One swift tug and the rashie pulled up over her head and landed on the floor amongst the other bits of mess and neglect. For a nanosecond, all those drills about safety itched her good sense, she knew she should keep the rashie on for body warmth, but she suppressed it with an angry shudder and resumed wrestling her suit on.

The hip swivel dance of donning a damp wetsuit might have gone easier with music rather than angry verbal explosions, but eventually she managed to tug it over her abdomen, jumping up and down, smoothing out the wrinkles and dragging it over her bare breasts. The arms proved just as difficult as the legs. She rubbed lubricant on her hands, wrists, and forearms, and pushed into one sleeve tube and then the other. The struggle kept her warm enough not to notice the rapid drop in temperature. Twisting like a pretzel, Cassie tried to catch the long zip-pull at the back of her suit. The anger simmering in her gut flared up again.

"I told them I needed a new friggin' suit. It's too small, I can't move in this mongrel thing. Oh right, I'm not entitled to one because . . . I DON'T CARE!" Her shout filled the room.

A sudden lurch of the houseboat flipped the zip-pull into her grasping palm.

"Finally."

Tugging the zip up to her neck, she fastened the suit firmly around her throat.

She swung her arms up and out, and side to side,

testing the material for flexibility, mumbling a litany of curses at the restriction.

"They could have sent a bloody email at least. How much time does it take to send an email? It's not as if I want a big song and dance with a gaudily wrapped gift. No, they are too busy kissing some stinking forest rat back to life to say *happy birthday* to their own daughter."

She slapped open her wardrobe doors and stood holding them against the constant movement of the houseboat. She stared at the old map of Melbourne from before the rising of the water levels. Letting go of one door, she moved her fingertip around a few of the pins in the map, then tapped her lips.

I need more plastic. I could trade out of here if I had enough, get a life where I never have to think about them again. Nothing worth finding north, it's all been picked clean in that direction. Maybe east? I'll go east.

Her finger followed the line she had drawn, of the outer perimeter wall, until it reached just north of the Toorak residential moorings. She tapped a small x on the map. Her mouth turned up in a half-smile.

Spend enough time on the perimeter and look what we find, a little hole in the defences just big enough for me to sneak out. Luckily I haven't told anyone yet or I would be stuck here for the rest of the day. If I get there without being stopped, I'm spending my birthday dancing with the fishes.

Which proved easier and harder than expected. Cassie fought the wind and choppy waves all the way to the inner perimeter and avoided meeting anyone in the first downpour. She made it to the closest dive equipment shed and selected gear for a deep dive. Shrugging off a twinge of guilt, she wrote in the equipment log and signed it.

No one will even notice I'm gone in this weather. I bet they are all curled around hot mugs playing cards somewhere. It's not as if anyone would celebrate my birthday anyway.

She secured the door and made her way to the outer perimeter wall.

She hesitated.

Thunder rumbled ominously. The temperature had been dropping steadily all morning. Waves hit the concrete barrier with hefty slaps.

Shivering in the cold, Cassie let the last embers of her anger choose her path.

It'll be warmer down below.

Cassie dropped into the water, kicking across the turbulent shallows on the tops of the buildings closest to the outer wall. Buffeted by the push and pull of the waves, she reached the edge and dived deeper into one of the roadways submerged between the reefs that had once been houses and shops.

An hour of hard swimming and she barely cleared

the last of the artificial reef. Her legs and arms felt leaden and her anger had long since dissolved in the sea leaving only a dangerous level of exhaustion. Just as she decided to turn back, a flash of light illuminated her surroundings.

Is someone else down here with a torch?

She twisted around, looking for another diver. A flash, brighter than the last, cut through the building gloom. Sand and debris had been kicked up in the storm agitated water, clouding the surrounding sea. Cassie felt a sense of dread.

But it's too cold for lightning to hit the water.

A giant invisible hand grabbed her in a vice-like grip. All of the anger that had simmered in her throughout the day seemed to manifest into this violent compression pushing her down. Every part of her body from the webbing between her fingers to the bases of her feet felt squashed.

Another flash came with intense heat and equally intense pain, and then there was nothing.

CHAPTER THREE

The girl moaned in pain, sweat patterning her brow. A woman fanned air across the sweat to cool her. The girl remained oblivious to the three people looking at her: an old woman, a younger man, and a child hiding behind a well-worn armchair pushed against the canvas wall.

The old woman watched her leader pacing across the limited floor space of her tent, made more limited by the canvas camp bed in the middle of the floor. He ran a working man's hand through his tousled hair and chewed his bottom lip. She waited quietly for him to reach a decision.

"We can't afford another mouth right now. Resources are stretched thin, you know this, with the boy and his mother turning up last spring we are at capacity."

The woman nodded slowly and gently placed more pungent mud on the girl's shoulder. "Could we put her in the storage shed? She's hurt bad but I can mend her with some time."

"There's not enough water. I can't get that damn thing to squeeze another drop out. I'm already rationing and we haven't got any worthwhile trade goods to bring in extra."

"I can give her half of mine. I'm old, I don't need a whole litre."

He pulled his hands down his face and groaned. "Don't do this to me, Aunty. She's probably never going to come good after taking a hit like that. We can't support her."

"That's what you said about Julie and look how much better off we are because of her."

"That's different. Julie can outwork most of us; being deaf doesn't stop her supporting herself. That girl, on the other hand, won't last a week. Look how soft she is. She's so full of water she'll die of thirst if that burn doesn't take her out before that."

The girl on the floor moaned in pain but didn't wake up. They both looked at her for a moment, then at each other.

He frowned at the old woman. She raised an eyebrow in question. He sighed, rubbing his palms up his face and into his hair, pushing it back from his forehead.

"Okay, she can stay. But don't give up your water, you need it—a litre isn't really enough for anyone. I'll find some for her and I'll sort a space in the shed."

"Good lad." The old lady reached up to pull his face down by the ears and kissed his forehead.

CHAPTER FOUR

Waking up hurt. Pain hammered inside Cassie's skull and down her limbs, but it was a pain that seemed familiar. The things that fully woke her consisted of a mixture of the pain, an incredible stench assaulting her nostrils, and thirst, roughly in that order. Thirst won first place in the push for her immediate attention.

"Water?" The word clawed its way past the arid surface of her throat and tongue.

"Get her some." A gruff but not unfriendly voice gave the order. Footsteps scurried to obey.

Cassie attempted to sit up, disgorging more stench from the blanket draped over her. Her instinct to push it away halted only as she realised she was naked underneath it. She wanted to yell a protest but no further words were willing to make the journey.

A dirty kid of about five or six, wearing what looked like a bundle of rags, handed over a tin cup. Cassie clutched at it and started to gulp the brackish brown liquid inside it. Just enough moisture freed her tongue before she flung the contents to the floor. The child gasped and scurried backwards.

"What the hell is that shit? Are you trying to poison me?"

"That *shit* is one-quarter of a daily ration of water. Don't give her any more until sundown, she might appreciate it by then." The gruff voice belonged to a tall man, maybe thirty, with squint wrinkles around his eyes. He pushed a lock of scruffy sun-bleached hair back from his forehead and spent a few moments intently surveying her.

Cassie clutched her blanket tight to her chin and stared back at him. "What are you looking at?"

He curled a corner of his mouth in a sneer, shaking his head. "A waste of a fortnight of good water."

"You call that good?" She pointed at the wet patch on the floorboards. "That stuff would kill fish."

"Perhaps, but it's all we have. The water plant's broken."

She pulled her head back and frowned. "Then fix it!"

He looked puzzled. "Where the hell did you come from that you assume someone can just fix things?" He didn't wait for her to answer and strode from the room, pulling the door hard behind him.

"Everyone can fix things at home," she whispered at his retreating back and pulled her knees up to her chest to rest her chin on, wincing at the pain.

The kid came back and looked her up and down in a miniature imitation of the man who had just left. "Why'd ya throw your water away? Are you stupid? Aunty says you probably lost your brains in the surf when the storm got you. Where ya from? Did you really swim in a storm? You must be really stupid."

The barrage of words from the kid reminded Cassie just how much her head was pounding. Cassie held up her palm toward the child in an attempt to stem the flow of noise. She rested her forehead in her other palm.

"Can I have some more water, please and is there any pain relief?"

"Nah. Boss says no more water cos you wasted it and we don't got no pain stuff unless it washes up. Aunty'll check on ya later."

The pain was too fierce for niceties. Cassie snapped at the kid, "How was I supposed to know your water plant can't bloody produce clean water? Where are my things? Why does this blanket stink?"

"Not s'posed to tell you nuffin' cos you're salvage and salvage is fair gain. It's the dog's blanket and she's agro that you got it, we don't get many blankets to spare. Aunty'll git ya somethin' to wear later." The child flashed a cheeky grin and waved a small hand up and down. "Go back to sleep, it'll make the time go fast and Aunty says you got a lot of healing to do. You know, so you're not worthless."

"Worthless? I'm not worthless! Clear off you little monster."

The kid shrugged and followed the gruff man through the door.

Trying to ignore the pounding in her head and the urgent need to moisten her parched throat, Cassie turned to look at her surroundings. The room was a patchwork of mismatched materials held with whatever could be found to tie it together. It was filled with crates and boxes, jars, bottles and containers of all colours, shapes, and sizes. They stacked in neat piles with just enough space cleared for her makeshift bed beside the only door.

She tried to roll on her side and cried out in pain.

What did that guy mean by a fortnight? Where am I? What the hell happened to me? "And where am I?"

"You're not in Kansas anymore, Toto." A very old woman with skin like leather came through the door holding a bundle of cloth and a tray with a pot of something that smelled as bad as the blanket.

"What?"

The woman chuckled "Sorry, that was silly of me, you're too young to remember that old movie. Heck, I'm too young to remember it, but I did see it once a long time ago—it's about a girl who gets blown away from home . . . Oh, never mind. I'm Winnie, Aunty to most of the people around here. What's your name?"

"Cassie."

"Well, Cassie, it's lovely to meet you dear, even if the circumstances are not ideal. I mean, we already met but you haven't been with us much these past few weeks. In the old days they would have had you up and about in no time. Now I'm the closest we have to a doctor, better than a doctor, really, because we use the old medicines."

"You mean pre-Rise medicines?"

The woman chuckled again and waved a hand in dismissal. "Every now and then some of the pre-Rise stuff washes up, mostly useless but I'm talking about the medicine my ancestors used, the really old medicine. They do take a bit longer because they work with your body, though you may have some nasty scars from the burns and your skin will be sensitive for a long time."

"Burns? How did I . . . ?" Cassie tried to twist to see over her shoulder. The scent of the ointment made her gag.

"We think you were hit by lightning out there in the storm. Probably hit your tank, which is why you survived, but you can't survive a thing like that without damage. What were you thinking, going diving in a storm like that? Never mind, don't fret. Here, drink this. I boiled it and put it through some cloth."

This time the water was cleaner, and Cassie gulped it down, trying to ignore the rusty aftertaste.

"Now this is going to hurt, but it must be done."

Cassie screamed as Aunty touched her shoulder. Sweat broke out on her forehead as blood drained from her head in a clammy reaction. The world took on a grey tone before winking out.

CHAPTER FIVE

"Is the girl asleep?" A woman in the group of people gathered in the shed nodded at the bedding.

Cassie kept the blanket over her head and remained still.

The gruff man seemed to be their leader. He looked across at the bed, shrugged and turned back to the group. Through a small hole in the blanket she watched him slip something in his mouth and suck on it, and her throat reacted in longing. He held a notepad and stylus and jotted notes as the others came up with suggestions for generating some trade which seemed to be the topic of the meeting.

"We have enough in the stores to get us through winter, Glen, but it'll be tight unless we get a good haul in the next storm. We could trade those bolts of cloth. They're dry now and mildew free."

The stylus tapped the screen and added the information. Then Glen turned to two women on his right. "How's the diving equipment coming on? Having two tanks means we can dive for the big stuff at last."

"We're working on it. It's looking promising. We should be able to take it down to the beach and try it tomorrow once the sun powers the battery up enough for the compressor."

"Stroke of luck that girl washing up," someone added.

Some in the group nodded agreement but no one smiled. *My diving gear? What's wrong with my diving equipment? How badly did the lightning damage it?*

"I'll dive first. I'm not risking any of you if it's faulty equipment." Glen's tone brooked no opposition.

"How is the lass, Glen?"

"She'll make it, thanks to Aunty, but we don't know if she'll be a few fish short of a haul or if she'll be able to work her credit balance off, but that's a worry for tomorrow. What else can we trade to get some water? Have we heard back from New Melbourne if they can send someone out?"

"You know we can't afford those elitist bastards. It has to be a catastrophe for them to send out someone with tech skills."

Elitist bastards? We aren't elitists. Surely New Melbourne will help? They need that water plant working, that's what they train us all for, isn't it?

"Or we'd have to have a wee marsupial on the brink of extinction to get them to even notice we exist. Don't hold your breath waiting for them, lad."

Cassie felt sick. This was something she needed to think about. She was so puzzled by what she was hearing but the ever-present pain made it difficult to catch her thoughts.

Glen nodded, slapped his forehead and laughed. "You're right. What was I thinking? Back to reality. . ."

Surely someone will come to help them, they have no water. When they come they can take me home . . . they will take me home . . .

Cassie closed her eyes. It was easier to sleep than think. She missed the rest of the meeting.

CHAPTER SIX

Cassie surfaced from nightmares of huge waves and pain. She lay panting in the dark, her bladder screaming protests at her. Her first attempt to sit up almost sent her back into nightmares, but slowly she managed to get upright. Trying to orient herself to her memory of where things were stacked and where the door might be, she took small steps and swayed.

What's wrong with the floor?

The whole place felt like it was rocking under her feet.

Is this what land legs feels like?

Tentatively, she moved forward with arms outstretched until she felt the shape of the door. She patted the wall beside the door trying to locate a light switch.

Someone snickered. She spun around and pressed her back to the door.

"Who's there?"

"It's me." The voice belonged to the kid. "Glen said I had to keep watch and tell Aunty when you woke up. You won't find no light switches here, if that's what you're lookin' for. We got technol . . . technol . . . the lights come on at night and stay on till they run out of sunlight. You got wobbly legs? You must've come off the sea. Did ya live in a boat or somefing?"

"No." A sense of self-preservation stopped her telling this child anything that was sure to be reported back and she had no way of knowing what these people wanted from her. "No, I didn't live in a boat. What's wrong with your battery storage?"

"I dunno? No room for it in our tents and we mostly don't use the shed at night."

The kid shoved her to one side of the door and a slightly less dark oblong of night sky appeared in the enclosed darkness of the shed.

"Where's the battery?"

"The dunny is this way."

"The toilet can wait, show me the battery. I want lights and I'm in too much pain to be stumbling over crap, okay?"

"Okay Grumpy, it's 'round here. If you wee yourself it's not my fault!"

They walked around the shed in the dark, touching the walls until they encountered a box. Cassie felt around the sides and up the wall above the box, clutching her blanket to her chest with one hand and mumbling in non-stop irritation.

"I need a light. There should be a light in here. What is wrong with you people? Why would you not have lights if the equipment is here? Are all mainlanders this useless?"

Cassie tugged open the cover and felt around for the emergency light. Cobwebs festooned her fingers.

"Ew, oh yuck, there better not be a redback in here. I don't want to die. Who does your maintenance? Or should I say, doesn't do?"

"What's a mainlander? Whatcha lookin' for? Can ya fix it?" The kid's voice floated out of the darkness near her hip.

"Doesn't matter." Cassie rubbed her fingers down the blanket and shifted most of the sticky webbing. She tugged the slipping blanket back up before feeling along the gauge panel. Her fingers touched a small lightbulb. It sat loose in its socket. She screwed it in and a yellow gleam, barely bright enough to illuminate her hand, lit up the inside of the box. Cassie jumped back and shuddered.

She gulped a few times and in a quavering voice demanded, "Find me a stick, kid."

A few minutes later she took the proffered stick and scraped out years of a well-established spider community. Spiders crawled rapidly over the sides of the box and disappeared into the dark beyond the circle of dull yellow light. She threw the stick with its ball of webbing as far as her pain would allow and turned back to the box.

"So, no one does your maintenance then." Cassie muttered a further string of quiet profanities as she checked the neglected state of the storage unit. "Too close to the sea . . . should've used more plastic . . . damn corrosion . . . this is still intact, that's a good sign . . . if I just twist this . . . and this can reroute to here . . . and that's it . . . okay, kid, where's the toilet?"

She snapped the cover back on with a satisfying click. The kid grabbed Cassie's wrist and dragged her away from the hut toward some indistinct dark mounds. Cassie clutched her blanket and stumbled along the unfamiliar sandy track.

"Will all the lights work? Even the one in the dunny? I hate goin' at night. Nearly everybody's asleep so you'll be able to do your business in private. Glen says you probably don't like people looking."

"Almighty Glen doesn't know anything about me,"

Cassie huffed, "but he's right about that." She shuddered at the thought of having no privacy.

They stopped at a narrow wooden structure nestled against a looming sand dune. Her eyes had adjusted enough to make out plants on the pale sand. The darkness inside the little wooden house contained a well-worn wooden seat with a hole in the middle.

"I dunno how youse do it where you come from but we usually walk down to the beach and wash our bums. It used to have a washy squirty thing but we don't got nobody what can fix it. I can take ya down after ya finish. Aunty says you should go for a swim and get clean anyway 'cause you stink."

***

The plunge into the predawn chilly water felt amazing except for the powerful sting across her healing burn. Scrubbing with handfuls of wet sand, Cassie sluiced off the stench of her recuperation and confinement. She floated on the water, gently bobbing up and down with the waves, and watched the sky changing colour.

"Come on." Something hit the water near her head, a splash to catch her attention. She rolled onto her front to see the kid waving at her from the beach. She took her time swimming into the shallow water, then ran to grab her blanket and wrap it around as fast as she could. She wrinkled her nose at the stench and realised it had been her making the blanket stink.

A tall man, Glen she assumed, stood cross-armed on the top of the dune. He gave the impression he was made of rock with his solid presence. He studied the sky intently, making Cassie look up to see what he was looking at. Blood red clouds against the washed-out blue gave her the same information he was gathering. More storms were on the horizon. Glen looked down at the beach and acknowledged the kid waving with some odd waving of his own.

"Glen says to get you fed and dressed. Aunty has some clothes for you."

"How do you know all that?"

"He just tol' me." The kid opened both palms and shrugged as if that should be enough information, turned and scampered back up the path.

The path was easier to negotiate in the dawn light. The dark lumps of the earlier trip turned out to be tents nestled into the dune sands. They stopped at one of the bigger ones.

"There you are, Mouse. Just in time for breakfast as usual. Good morning, Cassie. Do you feel better after a swim? It's always good to feel clean. Here, get dressed, you will feel so much more civilised with clothes on."

Civilised? Civilised is a hot shower and my own bed.

The bundle of clothes Aunty handed her contained jeans, a tee-shirt, and underwear. Cassie pulled on the undies with her back to the kid and Aunty. The bra felt too tight and she had to leave the strap off her shoulder, the undies a bit loose, the jeans fit snug and the shirt was meant for a much larger person, but they were clean. Hot tears pushed at her lashes. She took a few deep breaths to quell them before turning around.

"Perfect, thank you."

"Sit, sit, both of you."

They sat on cushions in the middle of the floor. The tent had bunches of herbs hanging from the main roof strut, a small dresser filled with pots and jars, and piles of books along one wall. A hammock swung on one side of the tent opposite the entrance flaps. The whole structure seemed sturdy and permanent. Aunty handed over plates with eggs and salad and a round flatbread.

"Now, Glen wants me to find out a bit about you, Cassie, and for me to tell you about us. Let's see how we can help each other. What will make your salvage worthwhile?"

Cassie stopped eating and stared at the old woman. "What are you talking about? I'm a person, not a thing. I can't be salvage . . ."

"Of course you are, we pulled you out of the sea."

Aunty handed Mouse another egg.

All the little clues dropped into place. Cassie felt her mouth go drier than it had been and the blood drained from her face. "Are you Combers?"

Killers? Lawless? Territorial?

"Yes dear, we are the Melton Combers and anything that washes up on our beach is salvage to us. It is lucky you washed up in our territory."

Lucky? I'm having breakfast with killers, how is that lucky?

"You look quite pale, Cassie—have a sip of tea, it will help."

"It said on the news that you . . . the Melton Combers, that you . . ." Cassie's hands shook. She curled them tight in her lap.

"On the news was it, my goodness. What was on the news?"

Cassie's voice came out in a squeak. "You killed three people on the beach."

Aunty stared for a long moment, then her whole body wobbled with her laughter. Mouse joined her.

"Never killed anyone in my life. Have you killed anyone, Mouse?" Aunty wiped tears from her cheeks with the back of her hand. Mouse kept laughing. "Glen keeps a tight rein on our gang and he won't stand for violence."

"But the news said . . ."

"Maybe you should find out the facts before you jump to conclusions about us." Aunty handed a steaming mug to Cassie.

Mouse sat up and stared at her, the laughter replaced with a fierce frown. "Glen's the best leader, he looks out for us. Don't you say bad things about Glen. It wasn't us what killed them people."

Cassie's eyes widened and her stomach knotted. "So people were killed?"

"It was the Airporters." Mouse's little fists pounded on skinny knees. Fierce loyalty shone from the determined face turned up to Cassie's.

"Yes." Aunty grabbed the little fists and held them still. "But it *was* on our territory. As I said, it's lucky you washed up here. Some of the gangs would've thrown you to the sharks rather than fix you up. Or worse."

What's worse than being thrown to sharks?

"Now, what were we talking about? Oh yes, what can you do?"

How much do I really want them to know about me? People who keep others as salvage? It's barbaric. Maybe they didn't kill anyone, but how do I know they wouldn't?

"I'm good at teamwork." Cassie spoke slowly and counted on her fingers. "I learn things quickly and I don't need to be shown more than once or twice. I'm a bit messy and forget to stow things away."

"Stow, you say. Did you live on a ship before this?"

"No, I never lived on a ship. I'm really hungry." Cassie filled her mouth with salad greens.

"That just proves you are healing. It's a good sign."

A familiar gruff voice called from outside, "May I enter, Aunty?"

"Of course, Glen, just in time for breakfast. If Mouse has left you anything."

Glen bent to come through the tent flap and folded himself onto a cushion beside Cassie. He ruffled Mouse's hair and reached for some flatbread. Cassie could feel the heat of him where his arm brushed hers. The salad greens clogged her mouth.

"Good morning, Cassie. Are you feeling better today?" He moved his hands in odd ways as he spoke to her. She was fascinated by the fluid movement of his fingers, almost as if they were dancing.

"Mmmmyef fangoo." She tried to swallow the greens and began to choke. Mouse thumped her on the back and she sprayed half-chewed leaves across the floor. Wiping saliva off her chin, the heat of embarrassment coated her cheeks as she scrambled to collect what she could. "I'm so sorry, Aunty."

Glen started to laugh, a warm honey laugh and slapped her on the back too, not quite as hard as Mouse had. She coughed again and dislodged a hidden leaf which made him laugh harder. Aunty and Mouse joined in until Cassie could not resist and began to laugh too.

"That was so embarrassing. I don't usually spit my breakfast at people. Um, where can I put this?" She dropped a handful of partly chewed leaves into the compost pot Aunty handed her. She surreptitiously wiped her hands on her jeans.

"Don't worry about it. It's good to hear you laugh, even if you are still throwing things around, or spitting them, I should say." His eyes held as much laughter as his mouth.

She returned his smile, not feeling any judgement in his words.

"Welcome to the Melton Combers. What would you like to know about us?"

"Why do you live like this?" She gestured around her.

"Like what? In tents? On the beach? As Combers?"

"Yes."

His face friendly and open, Glen laughed softly. He pushed a loose lock of hair back from his face.

"Okay, short version, living in tents is freedom. If we lived in the cities we would have to live by their laws. Every place, as you know, has its own set of rules. Here we set our own. There are laws of salvage and most of the Combers abide by them, but not always. We salvage because there is still so much being washed up out of the old city and on the tides from around the world, we can trade it inland for things we need. Most of us were salvage of some kind, drifting in from other places where we didn't belong. Do you want that last piece of bread?"

Cassie shook her head and Glen spread some fruit puree on it, curled it up and pushed it into his mouth. Cassie smiled, reminded of Vince at breakfast before school when they were kids.

"They used to have a central government who oversaw the whole country, before the Rise, can you believe that?"

Cassie nodded, she knew a fair bit of pre-Rise history from her Granddad.

"How can anyone know from far away what people need? It's not a bad life, being a Comber. Pretty cold in winter some years, but we get by. Now, what about you? What's your story?"

"Nothing," Cassie said quietly, staring into her cup. "I'm not anything, not important to anyone, I just work at what I'm told to do. I don't do anything much. I made a seriously bad decision to dive alone in a storm and it landed me here. I doubt I am going to be any use to you at all." Cassie twisted one hand in her shirt hem and kept her eyes on the pattern of the woven mat they were sitting on. "They won't waste resources finding one damn fool like me." She whispered the last words.

Glen looked hard at her for a moment and all the laughter left his face. He waved his hands in that odd way. Aunty nodded.

"I am sure we can find something you can do. As our salvage you are part of Melton Combers now. We'll find a way for you to work off your credit balance. Now I'm sorry Cassie . . ."

Credit balance? What does that mean, exactly?

"Mouse,"—Glen put his hand on the child's shoulder—"I need to talk to Aunty. Would you mind heading back to the shed for now?"

"I'll take Cassie back, Glen. She's got wobbly sea legs."

Glen held the tent flap open for Cassie and Mouse to go through and dropped it back after them.

Cassie lingered outside, resisting Mouse's urging to move.

"What's she not telling us, Aunty? Did you get anything out of her?"

Mouse tugged at her sleeve and tried to pull her away.

"No more than you did, lad. She seems to think we're murderers and slavers. Apparently it was on the 'news'. How fancy is that?" Aunty chuckled softly.

"Do you listen to the other channels?"

Cassie narrowed her eyes and resisted as Mouse changed from pulling to pushing in an attempt to shift her.

Did I see an antique radio on that dresser?

"The batteries are getting too hard to source, Glen. I've got a few left from your last trip to Echuca but they are not going to last much longer. We could try and rig a solar panel to it. And yes, I do listen to the other channels now-and-then, in all that leisure time I have." She laughed. "I miss the music. We need more music but I know, I know, we need the weather information more. If that solar battery in the shed worked we could hook the radio up in there and run it all day, then we could have music, weather and 'news'."

"I'll put it on the wish list, Aunty. Thanks for breakfast."

Cassie allowed Mouse to move her away from the tent before Glen caught her listening.

CHAPTER SEVEN

On the way back to the storage shed, Cassie stopped by a roofed cage containing a machine with multiple gauges, lots of small tubes and several large ones going into the ground. The door was not locked so she opened it. Reaching in, she tapped a few glass fronts and jiggled some connectors.

"Is this the desal water purifier for all of you?"

"Yeah, but it's stuffed. That's why the water is brown."

"Can you find me some tools, Mouse?"

"Not s'posed to let you touch stuff, but do ya reckon you can fix it too?"

"If you get me tools, I'll have a go at it. I'm not drinking another drop of that filthy stuff you consider water."

A sweaty hour later, Cassie dropped the last spanner into the toolbox and handed it to Mouse. She wiped the back of her hand across her forehead and smiled. Patting the metal side of the desal plant, she flipped a switch and the thing began to gurgle, then cough and splutter. Cassie put the backs of her knuckles on her hips and frowned. Finally, the gurgle, cough, splutter settled into a regular deep rhythm. She let out a breath she wasn't aware she had been holding.

"That should do it. It'll take a while for the system to flush, but the water will be crystal clear this time tomorrow."

She locked the door of the cage and followed Mouse on still wobbly legs.

***

Cassie rested for about an hour when Mouse came to take her back to Aunty's tent.

"I just want to check your shoulder dear, before the morning gets away from us. Why don't you ask me questions this time? Maybe I can set your mind at ease about your situation."

Aunty expertly checked the wound and covered it with a fresh layer of the pungent mud.

"Okay, how can you keep people as salvage? How? It's not right or decent."

"We don't keep people—everyone is here of their own free will. But if you wash up on our shore with nothing to your name, do you expect people to house and feed you for nothing? Is that right or fair?"

"At home we . . ."

We all share everything, food, housing, work, education, everything. No one went without, no one had to . . .

"Whatever you did in your old home, that isn't here. Everything is limited here." Aunty gently patted Cassie's hand. "There is barely enough for us to survive. As salvage, you get to earn your keep and pay your way and then free yourself from debt to our mob for finding and fixing you. Not all Combers go by those rules as we told you at breakfast, but that's how we do it. You owe us, you pay it back. It's a fair exchange."

The tent flap opened and a woman stuck her head through. "Aunty, Glen says the big storm is almost on us and Mirvy has gone into labour. Also, can that new girl pull yet?"

Aunty stood and quickly gathering items into a woven bag. "I'll be with Mirvy in a few minutes. Mouse, go with Cassie to the shed, find her a coat and get her down to the beach. Cassie, you are not to pull with your right arm dear, only your left. Do what you can and do what Glen tells you if he is back. Mouse will let you know who is in charge if he isn't. Here, take this water bottle and keep it safe. Mouse, watch out for her, she won't know the ropes."

Aunty ducked out of the tent and the other women held the flap until Cassie and Mouse were through, then fastened it behind them and moved away.

***

Mouse found an oilskin coat in a rainbow rack of coats and jackets.

"This old stuff is better for keeping you dry than the new things. The plastic ones are really strong but they feel yuck when they get wet. The hemp ones are light and nearly as good as the oil ones, but put this on."

Cassie shrugged into the heavy brown coat with an intense amount of pain in her shoulder until the fabric stopped moving and the pain settled into the permanent fixture it had been for the past few weeks. "I need pain relief."

"Well, you gotta hope some washes up in the storm. We have to check all the nets before it hits and make sure the storage trolleys are oiled. You stick with me. You get a cut of whatever you bring in. I really want some good plastic. You clip your drink bottle on with this. Come on, we're late."

Mouse handed her a metal snap clip and watched to make sure Cassie put it on correctly.

"Everything you got, like the clothes and stuff, will come off your credits, but you can earn it back if you're quick. Come on, come on, we'll be late."

Mouse half-dragged Cassie down to the beach where a crowd had gathered. People were mending nets, attaching floats and checking over their equipment. They stopped and looked at her as she passed, nodding or calling greetings to Mouse.

"How's the new girl, Mouse? Can she work nets?"

"Dunno, Gumpy. She's still burned, hurts lots probably but she's not a whinger. She can do oiling, I reckon. Is Glen back?" Not waiting for a reply, Mouse ran off and left Cassie with Gumpy, a solid man in his mid-fifties.

Gumpy handed Cassie an oil can and showed her how to oil the wheels of the long row of trolleys lined up along the edge of the sand. She looked at him, then back at the can, and knelt in the sand to begin the task.

I'm in too much pain to think clearly. What happened to me out there? Was I really lucky I ended up here? How the hell am I going to get home? What did they do with my wetsuit and gear? Maybe it's better if they think I'm stupid? I just want to go home.

Her mind a turmoil of questions, Cassie moved

from trolley to trolley, oiling any moving part in the swift and efficient manner she had learned at home. It was no different than getting ready for a storm there and she quickly finished. She looked at the other tasks and joined in mending nets. People moved aside to let her in and watched until they saw she knew what she was doing and left her to work. The nets were well cared for and repairs were swiftly dealt with which gave her space to simply listen while they worked.

"The crew came back okay?"

"Yeah, but Glen almost left Rabbit behind."

"What? I'll string him up . . ." The outrage had an edge of humour in it, as if the person didn't believe Glen would leave someone behind.

"He got too cold, almost couldn't get in the boat. They had to haul him in. My Ron says he was shivering so much he couldn't grip the sides and wasn't thinking straight."

"Dumb arse. Did the new tank hold okay?"

"It's fine, they did an incredible job. It's a wonder that girl survived at all."

Cassie realised they had forgotten she was sitting with them.

"They managed to connect a dozen buoys we can collect when it's calm again. It should be a huge haul."

"Andy said Glen tried to convince them all to go

down for another dive." There were gasps of shock and some laughter.

"Idiot." It was said fondly.

"But then Andy wanted to get back and check on Mirvy before the storm."

"Fair enough, too."

"I think I am beginning to like this Glen of yours." Cassie had worked up the courage to speak, but a gust of wind tore her words up so no one noticed what she said.

Someone came around with mugs of hot drink and a bread she had never seen before. It had more of the fruit puree on it.

"This is delicious, what is it?"

"Where do you come from?" Several people laughed.

"It's damper. Don't you have damper at your place?" Mouse dropped down beside her and licked the fruit puree from sticky fingertips.

"No, we don't eat grain. We don't have the space to grow it. We use seaweed."

"Yuck."

"I like it. It has all the nutrition we need."

"Seaweed stinks." Mouse leapt up and danced away with excitement and anticipation energised by the oncoming storm.

The wind had turned the beach to sandblasting.

Everyone sat with their backs to the ocean just below the top of the dunes. Any conversation directed at Cassie was short and conducted through gritted teeth or bandanas to keep the sand out of their mouths.

"Why don't we take shelter?" Cassie raised her voice to be heard over the wind.

The woman beside her frowned, then shrugged. "What for? Half the tents will be down and we need to be on the beach as soon as stuff starts to surface. We can't leave anything for rival gangs to raid. Glen and the team were already out there marking lagan for retrieval; it's good that new scuba tank held up."

"What's lagan?"

"Goods thrown overboard s'posed to be marked with a buoy for picking up later, but the ships and cities never come back for it. We've been wanting to mark all that jettisoned cargo for a long time but Glen wouldn't let us do a solo dive with only one tank. He said it was too dangerous and he didn't want to lose anyone for a box of trinkets." The woman chewed her last mouthful and began waving to someone.

Cassie felt restless and cold sitting outside waiting for a storm to hit. Wet weather was for sitting inside reading or doing some craft, snacking and watching a movie and enjoying the rain washing down the outside of the window. She tapped the woman's arm and yelled into the wind, "What are we all waiting for?"

The woman pointed a thumb behind her in the direction of the water. "The storm has been driving flotsam and jetsam towards us. It'll start to come into the beach soon and if we are really lucky some of the derelict bits at the bottom of the ocean will get pushed up, too. That doesn't happen too often, but when it does we can land big winnings. The storm might have smashed a house and dislodged its contents. We'll get something cast aside by a city. They waste so much. I'm hoping for some plastic to trade. Good melting plastic is good credit. Hope your first Combing is plentiful."

Some silent signal electrified the gang and people scrambled over the dune and down to the beach.

The rain came straight at them filled with sand and pushed by a fierce wind. Putting their heads down, they pushed against it. Some went into the water and others stretched out nets between them.

Cassie blinked rapidly to keep the water and sand out of her eyes. She noticed the ones in the water wearing wet suits and recognised her own on a smaller woman.

"Hey Mouse, how does everyone know what to do?"

"Sign language," Mouse yelled over the howl of the wind and the roar of the waves breaking heavily in front of them. "You'll learn. Don't just stand around, you'll get in trouble." Grabbing her wrist, he pointed to a pile of floating seaweed and yelled again, "Find stuff!"

"What sort of stuff?" she yelled back.

Mouse shoved a soft cloth bag with a long strap at her. "Everything. Anything. Not seaweed, okay!"

She looked at the bag in her hand and shrugged.

I don't have to do this but they did rescue me and I suppose I should do something to thank them. It's not as if anyone is available to row me out to the city right now and I better get my things back to take home. I'll talk to Glen when he gets back, he seems like a reasonable person. Fossicking on the beach in a howling storm might be fun.

CHAPTER EIGHT

For the next few hours, Cassie worked hard to find things as the storm grew wilder. Mouse had long since disappeared into a team somewhere and the noise of the waves crashing made conversation impossible. With cold, stiff fingers, she filled her bag with a comb, empty bottles, plastic caps, plastic bowls, pieces of broken hard plastic, a wooden shoe, an egg-shaped rock, glasses frames, a mangled toothbrush—in fact, anything that she could pick up went into the bag. She felt hot inside the coat, but blissfully dry. The pain in her right shoulder had intensified.

Occasionally, she looked up to watch the Combers dragging the nets in, and—now that she was aware of it—Cassie could see them making hand signals to each other.

That's useful. Didn't we have a semester unit in sign language? I wonder if anyone at home actually uses it?

The wind had the people closer to shore bent double, while the ones further out disappeared behind enormous waves that rolled over them and crashed relentlessly onto the sand. The water pulled against those who held the nets in the shallows, sucking at their feet and legs with the powerful drag as it headed back out to sea. Cassie could barely keep her footing on the shore and the pain in her shoulder meant she would be useless pulling nets, so she moved further away to look for more stuff to fill her bag.

Lightning had been hitting the shore further down the beach so she headed in that direction, remembering reading about fulgurites forming when lightning discharges into the sand.

That might be something worth finding and they look awesome polished up.

The storm abated as she walked, but the wind continued just as fierce, making walking in a direct line challenging. The ocean roar filled her ears. People all along the waterline filled sacks at their sides. Some had three or four heavily laden bags but continued to shove things into them. Cassie picked up the odd piece missed or discarded by the Combers and kept walking.

She took little notice of several Combers moving in her direction from the far end of the beach. They all carried loaded bags. Cassie bent down to inspect a piece of coagulated sand and pulled it up to discover a corkscrew shape.

Corkscrew entry, now that's interesting.

She spotted another rock nearby and bent to inspect it. The sand had been solidified by the lightning into a rock-like construction. It was much larger than she anticipated and she focussed entirely on scooping sand away from the fulgurite, feeling the remnant of heat in the surrounding sand from the intensity of the energy that created it.

Darkness descended instantly. She pulled at the rough fabric over her face, her heart rattling against her rib cage. The weight of her collection bag disappeared as her body was hoisted from the ground and her head dropped. Her back landed with a thump against the back of whoever held her. A set of hard hands gripped her legs. Her face pushed against the tough fabric of the bag, making it impossible to scream for help. Her captor began to run, jolting her shoulder, mingling pain and terror making it difficult to breathe. Her brain switched off.

CHAPTER NINE

"I told'ya it was Cassie. She had to fight off a million zillion spiders and they went everywhere and she didn't even squeal and she said bad words but she did somefing to it." Mouse hopped from foot to foot, dancing around Glen as he stared into the gauge box of the power storage. He closed the cover with a firm click.

"It's working. It's bloody well working." His voice started on a whisper and rose to a shout. "Go tell Aunty to bring the radio up here."

Mouse took off, ragged coat flapping in the wind.

A few minutes later, Aunty made her way up the path, followed by Mouse tugging a small wagon with the radio perched in it. A crowd gathered to see what the shouting was about.

Glen propped the radio on the window ledge and plugged the cord into the socket in the gauge box. He flipped a switch, turned a dial, and music filled the air.

He turned and bowed to Aunty. "Your wish has been granted, my lady."

"You flamin' big galoot. How'd you get it working?" She slapped him on the arm.

"It was Cassie!" Mouse tried to shout over the music and the sudden burst of talk from a dozen different people. Mouse's shoulders drooped and five-year-old lips pouted. "Oooohwww, you never listen to me."

Glen ruffled Mouse's hair and squatted down to talk face-to-face. "Did Cassie do anything else?"

"I'm not gunna tell you cos you fink she ran away." Mouse lifted a determined chin and turned away.

"Hey Glen, come here. You've gotta see this." Rabbit waved him over.

"Sorry, Mouse. I'll be right back and you can not tell me then, okay?" Glen patted Mouse on the shoulder and jogged to the desal and purifier cage. "What's wrong now?"

"Nothing. Not a damn thing. Look."

Water was gushing from a tap. Clean, clear water in abundance. Glen put his palm under it and took a tentative sip. "What? How?" He cupped both hands in the flow and drank deeply.

Rabbit shook her head in wonder. "The whole system is working; intake, outflow, purifier, even the sewage. It's incredible. How did it happen?" Rabbit turned off the tap. "We can't get in for a close look though, someone locked the gate."

"You won't have to share your water ration anymore, Glen." Aunty slapped him on the arm and grinned.

"We won't have to ration at all, Aunty." He put an arm around her shoulders and hugged her.

Something tugged at Glen's sleeve. He looked down at Mouse. Mouse poked a cheeky tongue at him. "Will you listen now, huh?"

"Cassie did this?"

"Yep."

"More bad words?"

"Yep."

"You don't think she ran away?

"Nope."

"We better find her then."

CHAPTER TEN

Cassie woke from a nightmare of huge waves and deadly claws reaching, reaching, reaching for her.

She gasped for breath.

"Water." The word forced its way from her mouth.

"Tell the boss the salvage is awake."

Cassie heard feet running but couldn't see anything from where she lay. A haphazard pile of driftwood, threatening to topple over her if she moved too much, blocked her view. Her hands and feet were trapped. She lay on her right side and waves of pain throbbed through her. She whimpered, unable to contain the noise.

"Did one of you idiots break the merchandise?" This voice held a smooth, dangerous note.

"No boss, we think she was already damaged. She

must be new, her bag was full of useless shit like bottle caps and bits of rock."

"Hmmm, it's not like them. Perhaps this one has hidden value? Do you?"

A boot nudged the base of her foot and Cassie moaned at the ricochet of pain travelling up her body.

"Do you have any value?" Another kick with a boot, a bit harder this time.

"No." Cassie could barely find enough saliva in her mouth to get that one word out.

"Get water, I want to know why they kept her."

Someone pulled her head up by her hair and forced water into her mouth. Cassie gagged and sputtered but a hand clamped her mouth until she swallowed. Her head dropped back to the ground. The thud sent sparks through her brain.

"Untie her damned feet and sit her up. I can't question her like that, you idiots."

She wanted to scream at the blood rushing back to her feet but clamped her teeth down hard. The same hair-puller lifted her into a sitting position and propped her back against the driftwood.

The first thought on seeing the man in front of her was *pretentious.* The second thought, following close behind, *dangerous.* He sat in an ornate chair that was definitely pre-Rise by several centuries. His clothing looked to be the height of early 21ˢᵗ century rich boy: smooth classical lines to the suit, elegantly tailored to his exact fit, bright purple silk cravat and matching pocket kerchief, and a pair of the shiniest black leather boots with a bright silver buckle. A small marquee was erected over him to keep the rain off. Four henchmen—and they could only be henchmen with muscles on their muscles and low foreheads over jutting jaws—held down the legs of the marquee against the wind.

"I shall ask you some questions. If you answer them to my satisfaction, I will give you some water and perhaps allow you to be fed. If you do not answer to my satisfaction, I will think of some way to elicit the responses. First, who are you?"

He held up a long, thin hand and pulled back on one finger.

"Secondly, where are you from?" He pulled back on the second long, spindly finger.

"Third, what value do you have to the Combers from whom we acquired you?" He pulled back on the third stick finger, then leaned forward to hear her.

She looked at his face and thought it might have been beautiful, but there was something terrifying about his eyes.

"Well? I don't like to be kept waiting."

Everything in her screamed self-preservation. She

did not want this man knowing anything about her. "I washed up on the beach. I can't remember much, lightning hit me. They fixed me but took all my things. I think my things were valuable to them."

"What things, exactly?" The man sat with his elbows on the arms of the chair and his spindle fingers steepled in front of his chest.

"I was wearing a wetsuit and had a diving tank, mask and flippers when I washed up. The tank is probably wrecked because of the lightning. I was burncd."

"All the equipment for marking lagan. Hmm, I see. They could not simply jettison you because your equipment earned you credit. Yes, yes I see. You certainly don't look like a Comber, your skin is too . . ." He shook a hand in the air, trying to find the right description. "Oh, smooth. Your hair has seen a salon and you haven't eaten a lot of starch in your life. Most likely you came from a floating city. Who was in the area this past month?" The question was directed at a small bespectacled man with a book.

"Several large trade ships in at New Melbourne, sir, and Pansylvania City was nearby but did not come into range. Some small traders and desal boats."

"Hmm, not Pansylvania, she hasn't the correct lilt. Did you work on a boat?" He swung his face back to look at Cassie.

"I, I don't think so." *Let them think I've lost my memory.*

"I'm bored. If I throw her back into the sea, it will do the Melton Combers a favour, and we don't want that, do we. Or we could trade her. I want my dinner, I can't think on an empty stomach. Move." He stood and the henchmen lifted the marquee like a large, square umbrella. Someone else grabbed the chair and followed their leader away.

The weather hit Cassie full in the face as soon as the marquee shifted and she was grateful they hadn't stripped her coat from her. She curled into a ball against the driftwood, trying not to dislodge the stack, but it tumbled down anyway, completely covering her.

Better than being in the storm, I guess.

She tried to free her hands but they were tightly bound.

I'm good at knots, I'm very good at knots, but no-one ever suggested we learn how to undo wet knots we can't see. I want to go home.

She pushed her forehead into the cold sand and let a few tears drip down from her face. Her throat felt dry and a huge lump formed a lead ball in her chest. Water dripped constantly through the stack of wood.

Cassie turned her head and licked at a small pool

of rainwater on a piece of wood next to her. The salt content was too high to quench her thirst.

The light faded as night came on and she began shivering in the cold. Her stomach had stopped demanding food some hours ago.

Maybe they forgot about me. Maybe I could find my way back to the Melton Combers? I'm so cold. I have to move.

She kicked the boards and twisted around in her small, cramped space. The driftwood slid off as Cassie stood up. She couldn't see much. The surf pounding nearby gave her a partial orientation but she had no idea which direction they had come from or how far they had travelled. As her eyes adjusted, she noticed some light in the dunes and greater light in the distance which she assumed would be Melton City. She turned towards the ocean and squinted into the darkness, hoping to spot something that would tell her where home was.

She shook her head, spraying droplets from her wet hair. She sighed. A sense of futility filled her. If she could see New Melbourne, she couldn't get there, her hands were tied too tight, she didn't know how to find a boat and doubted she could row thirty kilometres in rough seas even if she could find one, and what if they turned her away if she did make it?

The Melton Combers were her best option. She began to walk in what she hoped was the right direction, stumbling over grass and hidden dips in the dunes, falling frequently but getting back up and trudging on.

A noise intruded on her thoughts. The thrum of a plane engine added an extra note to the heavy patter of rain.

I must be near the airport? Maybe I can find help there. I wish I'd listened in Politics and Borders class. Vince was right, I should have studied more. Vince, do you even know I'm missing? Do you care?

Cassie gave a self-deprecating snort and stumbled into a dip in the dunes. About to elbow her way back up, she froze.

"She can't get far with her hands tied. Find her before the boss finds out she's gone. Ten credits to the one who brings her back in one piece."

Beams of light flashed across the dunes, cutting lines in the darkness. Cassie crawled further into the dip and fell into a small creek. Her clothes soaked up water, even the oilskin absorbed water making it heavier than ever.

Dogs began to bark. Cassie's heart beat rapidly in response. She splashed along the creek bed and fell headlong into a deep pool. The oilskin dragged her under. Her hands useless behind her, panic seized her chest but she kept her head and held her breath.

Light played across the water above her for a long,

agonising moment, then moved on. Cassie felt the bottom of the pool and shoved with one foot, then the other, her lungs desperate for air. She moved toward what she hoped was the shallow water and her face finally broke the surface. Gulping in air as quietly as she could, she flopped into the mud on the bank.

The shivering intensified, a mixture of fear and cold. Another plane hummed into the night. Cassie lay still for a few minutes with her cheek in the mud, weeping silently.

Please, can I just wake up and all this will be a nightmare and I'll tell Vince so he laughs and puts me in a headlock. I want a seaweed roll. I want a big drink of clean water. I want my Mum and Dad. I wonder if they care that I'm gone. I wonder if they know I'm gone. Why is this all happening to me? I'm sorry. I'm so sorry. I don't know what I'm sorry for?

She lay in the mud a little longer.

Come on stupid, get off the ground and start moving before you die of hypothermia.

She pushed onto her knees and stood up awkwardly. One foot in the mud and one further up the bank, her thigh muscles tensing, she pushed herself slowly up the bank, using her elbows to steady herself. Just as she reached the top, a pair of meaty hands grabbed a handful of her hair and the lapels of her coat. A dog snout growled in her face.

"You just netted me some credit, girly. I think for that, I won't punch you for making me wet." The man twisted his fist tighter in her hair and hauled her upright, her scalp aching as he marched her back in the direction she had come.

They entered a large tent and he let go of her hair. She fell to the floor, muddy, soaking wet, her shoulders sagging.

The thin man sat in his antique chair, spinning something around in his fingers. His lips curled with distaste. He gagged a little and screwed up his nose.

"What a little adventure we've all had tonight. Hmmm? You are a dreadful sight and you are making my rug wet just like a dog. You smell like one too. Put her in the dog pen."

Cassie heard a few sudden intakes of breath. The man with the glasses spoke up. His voice soft and placating. "It will be difficult to trade her if she is dead, sir."

"Hmmm. All right, yes, those dogs are a bit rough. Put her in with the bitch instead. Just get the messy thing out of my sight. My Combers suggested she might be valuable; she had best be worth all this trouble."

Once again, Cassie was lifted to her feet by her hair. The pain was pulling up a shard of anger through the pervasive fear. "Why are you doing this to me? Are all you Combers monsters? How can you treat me like this? I never did anything to you. Let me go. Just let me go. I want to go home, this is a horrible place."

The thin man stopped spinning whatever it was in his hand and stared at her intently. "Now that is an interesting little outburst. Hmmm? *All you Combers . . .* What gives you the idea we are Combers?"

"In a tent, in the rain. Who else would live like this?"

"Live in a tent? Hmmm, how amusing. My dear, surely you know who I am?"

"I don't know and I don't care. You can't treat me like this. Let me go at once. You are violating my rights."

"Rights? How could anyone be that naive in today's world? Rights? A little gift bestowed by the society you live in. If you are lucky you assume you have them. That attitude only exists in one place, one tiny pocket of utopia. I think the stakes just went up, men."

A scuffle outside the tent caught everyone's attention. An angry voice demanded entry. Cassie recognised the gruff tones.

"Sir, the boss from the Melton gang wants to speak with you. Claims he wants his flotsam returned."

"Hmmm. The night gets more interesting by the second. Let him in."

Glen stepped in and filled the room in a way the

thin man could not. He looked at Cassie, taking in her purple swollen hands still tied at her back, her bedraggled state, the pool of water at her feet, the mud, and her hair tangled around the fingers of the man holding her up. His lips thinned for a moment, then he turned his attention directly to the Airport gang leader.

"Bryanth." Glen spoke the name like it was something filthy in his mouth. "You have my salvage and I have come to reclaim it."

"This is so unusual, Glen, you coming to collect instead of your subordinates. Hmmm? Very out of character."

"And you? What brings you slithering down here to the mud? Too quiet in your Airport?"

Bryanth lifted his chin and closed his eyes. His nostrils thinned and the corner of his top lip quivered for a moment as he drew in a long, slow breath. His eyes snapped open and looked straight at Glen. "Do you have proof she is yours? I feel there may be a prior claim."

"Witnessed and recorded. Her belongings converted to credit. Her current clothing and medical treatment balanced against it. She is mine and I am here to take her back. There is no prior claim."

Bryanth sat back with a smile on his face that made Cassie think of scavenger birds toying with live prey. He absently scratched the back of one long, thin hand with the nails on the other, spread his fingers wide and folded the fingers together, stilling his hands completely.

"I believe your claim should be for compensation from her original source, but I have contacted her people to trade her back." Bryanth stood and walked over to Cassie, pushing the tip of one fingertip against her forehead. "I do believe this little creature is from New Melbourne. They like to reclaim their own and I am sure this one will bring me great fortune."

Cassie fought against the hold in her hair and pulled free, stepping toward the two men negotiating for her. Bryanth leaned back in disgust; Glen held his ground.

"Who the hell are you two? What gives you the right to barter for me like I'm a flotsam that washed up? Shit!" Cassie dropped her voice and turned on Bryanth, grinding words out between her teeth. "You haven't had time to contact anyone since your thugs grabbed me off his beach." She jabbed her chin in Glen's direction. "And even if you had, they won't trade. They won't even be looking for me. It's policy not to waste resources for one fool who goes missing. Not even for me . . ." Her voice trailed off at the end.

One man's face became sympathetic, the other calculating. "Hmmm. Not even for you, hey? Who exactly are you, then?" Bryanth peered at her and Cassie imagined he would look at an interesting bug in a similar way.

"Just a crew member. I do maintenance and sewage duty, batten down the hatches with my team before a storm and clean up afterwards. I do garden duty and water duty and whatever other work they give me. I am just one cog in a machine, no more or less important than any other."

"Hmm. You said you were wearing dive equipment. Why would a lowly crew member be diving?"

"None of us are lowly. We are all equals." Cassie's shoulders and chin lifted unconsciously. "We all learn to dive and be on sal—underwater maintenance." Cassie bit her lip.

"Hmmm, salvage crews hey?"

"I said underwater maintenance. There is a lot of plumbing underwater."

"Glen, I cannot respond to your claim and will not return this salvage. I shall keep her right here until her people can trade for her. Hmmm? It's time you left, you are boring me." Bryanth waved the tips of his fingers in a dismissive gesture and spoke to the little man at his side. "Put her where I said she should be."

Glen hesitated and indicated Cassie with the palms of his hands. "Hell, Bryanth, at least free her hands. Any skill she has will be no good to trade without them."

Bryanth rolled his eyes and flapped a hand in Cassie's direction. "Oh for goodness sake, do as he says."

The henchman with a penchant for hair-pulling, produced a knife.

"Slowly! Do it slowly. Let me." Glen grabbed the knife before anyone could protest and knelt behind Cassie. He cut the rope enough to let some of the circulation back. Cassie moaned.

"This is ridiculous," Bryanth made a circle in the air to indicate Cassie and Glen then pointed at a henchman. "Watch them and lock her up as soon as prince charming frees her hands, then get him off my territory. I am bored and need to sleep."

Glen rubbed her hands gently and slowly eased the ropes off Cassie's wrists. The pain eclipsed the agony in her healing burns. He continued to rub her hands and hold her wrists as the colour changed from purple to her usual light tan. He whispered to her as he rubbed. "They'll be sore for a few days. I'm sorry I came so late. We thought you had run away."

"I've got nowhere on the mainland to run to."

"I understand that now. How did you fix . . . Okay, not the right time or place. We figured you had been grabbed when we found the fulgurite you half uncovered. It's not unusual for these scum to grab people on the beach, usually women or lads scavenging on their own.

We should've kept a closer eye on you. I'm so sorry. We'll do what we can. Try and keep your hopes up."

With that, he stood and left the tent, accompanied by two henchmen.

Keep my hopes up? I don't need hope, I need to get away from these monsters.

Cassie's hair was again twisted around the fat fingers of her guard. He led her out into the rain and walked her to the dog kennels. The males snarled and snapped at her for the whole length of their cages. She was shoved into the bitch enclosure. A soft growl sounded from the dark. Cassie sat with her back to the wall, her arms cradling her knees, and stayed as still as she could. Small yips came from what she assumed were puppies.

The growl continued for several minutes until the female seemed to decide that Cassie was no threat. Cassie started to cry and was soon wracked by sobs. A warm doggy nose pressed against her face and a rough tongue licked her cheeks. Cassie hugged the warm fur of the animal and pressed her face against the heat. The dog curled up beside her and lay its head in her lap. Cassie fell asleep in the comfort offered.

CHAPTER ELEVEN

"Since we are on such familiar terms, why don't you tell me your name?" Cassie held onto the meaty fingers in her hair in an attempt to alleviate the pain they were causing. The words squeezed out through her clamped teeth. She could barely keep up with the pace he set and was running on tiptoes, he was holding her so high.

"Harry." His voice was a rumble in his chest.

"Hairy?"

He reached his free hand around and pinched the soft skin under her upper arm, twisting it for good measure. Cassie squealed.

"I said Harry. My name is Harry."

"And is it your job to pull my hair like a toddler, Hairy?"

He kicked her in the back of the leg. She stumbled but he kept moving and she had to get her legs under her in spite of the pain.

"Harry. Say it right."

"Okay." Her leg throbbed, her arm hurt and her scalp had forgotten what it was supposed to feel like.

"Okay, Harry." He grabbed her wrist and squeezed it so hard she thought the bones would crack. "Say it."

"Okay, Hairy."

The punch caught her in the ribs, forcing all the air from her lungs. For a minute, she thought she would never be able to draw breath again.

What the fuck am I doing?

"Say it right! It's my name, how would you like it if people called you names? Say Harry!"

"Goodnight, Hairy."

Cassie discovered what a sentient punching bag might feel.

He threw her into the bitch's box and slammed the door.

"It's Harry."

The puppies licked her face and climbed over her, tugging at her clothes and hair. She reached out a hand and ruffled the fur of one. Their mother curled into Cassie's side. She could barely lift her arm to cuddle the dog.

"I must be insane, girl," Cassie whispered into the dog's fur, "What made me think I could provoke that stupid mountain and survive?

***

"Hmmm. You are very stupid, Harry. I said, keep her in line. I did not ask you to mangle her."

Bryanth looked at the bruised face of the girl crumpled at his feet. He flipped back the tails of his purple velvet cloak and walked around her with his hands clasped behind his back. He bent close to her face to inspect the array of bruises, then turned to look at his henchman.

"A thorough job, though I must say. It will prove useful when our would-be hero turns up again. What did you say provoked it?"

"She said my name wrong. She did it on purpose. She was annoying me."

"*Hmmm? Well you* are annoying *me*. How can I send her out for trade looking like this? Idiot!" Bryanth pulled a taser from his cloak and shoved it into Harry's abdomen. "Idiot! Idiot! Idiot! How many times must I tell you? Don't leave a visible mark. Do you understand?"

Harry lay on the floor whimpering, curled around his abdomen.

"Do you?" The taser discharged again and Harry's limbs jerked out straight. "Do you?" Again Harry spasmed.

The bespectacled man stepped forward. "Sir, I believe he understands. I will see to it he follows your instructions carefully."

"Hmmm? Oh good. I'm bored now." Bryanth dropped the taser onto the book the smaller man was holding. "Clean up in here. I do hate when they defecate like that."

Bryanth wafted from the room, a delicate piece of lace held to his nose.

Specs leaned over and whispered, "Please don't provoke him, Miss. No one can help you if you are dead."

Cassie squeezed open her least swollen eye and stared until he moved away.

***

Cassie watched the two men from the corner of the tent where her guard held her firmly by the hair.

This was the second time Glen had tried to negotiate for her return. She didn't hold much hope that the outcome would be any different.

"I demand under salvage rules that you return her to me." Glen's jaw worked to keep whatever else he wanted to say firmly in check.

"Hmmm. Now, why should I do that? Really, Glen. Could you of all people, have taken a shine to this little thing? What do you want with her?"

Glen looked at her bedraggled state, the filthy clothes she had been in for over a week, matted hair and the thick fingers twisting it into a short knotted rope to hold her in place. "Give her some clean clothes, or let her wash at least. This is revolting behaviour even for you. You're an animal." Glen's voice had risen until he yelled the final statement.

Bryanth giggled behind his cupped hands. "What a temper Glen, and in a rival territory, what is the world coming to. Hmmm? Where is your renowned even temper or your famous calm in a difficult negotiation? She shall have new clothes when she earns them. Doesn't she owe you for the clothes she is wearing? You can have them back when she gets new ones and I will trade you for her diving equipment."

"The equipment doesn't work. It was burned out when the lightning struck her."

"Hmmm? What a pity. Well, you can give it to me for scrap metal and I will give you her coat. I think that is fair, don't you?"

"No. She can keep the coat, we owe her that much . . ." Glen clamped his mouth on the rest of the sentence.

Bryanth sat forward in his chair. "Tell me more. I am eager to hear what you were going to say. Please, do go on, Glen." He sat up and waved his hands rapidly in a fanning motion. "No, don't tell me, let me guess." He held up a long thin index finger. "I think she fixed something for you. Did you fix something for him?" Bryanth looked from one to the other.

Cassie pulled against the hold in her hair and kicked a heel into Harry's shin. It earned her a strong heat-inducing tug against her scalp and his free hand grabbed the back of her neck.

"I didn't fix anything for *him*," she spat. "The tank is mine, not theirs. You can't trade my things."

Bryanth's smile slid up his face. He turned back to Glen, ignoring Cassie. "Oh, so she did fix something and I think the thing she fixed is a valuable commodity so she paid her debt to you and earned credit in doing so. Am I close? Oh yes, I see by the tic jumping in that chiselled jaw of yours that I am definitely on the right track. Oh, I do love to see you squirm, dear rival. It gives me tingly feels right here."

Bryanth dramatically arched his fingers over his heart, hiding another giggle behind his other hand, but he could not suppress the grin that spread past his fingertips. Then his face pulled into a tight cold mask.

"Unless you return with a trade offer I am willing to accept, I shall keep her, dress her, and house her as I see fit. Get off my territory, I'm bored now. Put her in with the dogs."

"I'm sorry, Cassie, I'll get help."

CHAPTER TWELVE

"Melbourne does not want you back."

Cassie forced herself not to show any reaction to Bryanth's statement. He looked at the small silver platter being held by Specs, a name Cassie silently attached to the smaller man since she had never heard a name for him.

Bryanth delicately picked a colourful sweet from the plate and held it up for inspection. Cassie watched him warily from her seat on the floor near his feet. He placed the item between his teeth and crunched it in half with a single snap of his jaw. The pieces flew across the tent, landing on opposite sides. "Hmmm. Perfect shot, don't you think?"

"Much further than last time, sir." Specs bowed

slightly, not moving the tray.

"Where was I? Hmmm? Yes, I was telling you that Melbourne does not want you back, so now you owe me the credit for your food and lodging."

Cassie clenched her teeth, feeling her jaw jut forward. She curled her hands into fists then relaxed them into her lap. She breathed slowly through her nostrils and tried to loosen her jaw.

"Good girl. You are not a slow learner. Let's see, where are we going to send you first?"

Specs gently placed the silver tray on a small table beside Bryanth's antique chair. He lifted a book and opened it to a book-marked page. "There is an electrical problem in Ballarat, sir. We have made contact with the city leaders and offered for this,"—he tilted the book for his boss to see—"and they will have her for three days."

"Hmmm? Make it happen. Harry stays with her at all times."

"Yes sir, of course." The small man bowed as his boss chose another sweet. "Shall I have her cleaned up for Ballarat, sir?"

"No. I like the way her disgusting state provokes the great do-gooder, and I'm sure he will be back."

Melbourne does not want me back? Not want me back? I can't go home?

Cassie swallowed back her tears.

***

Ballarat proved to be a simple job: Get the power grid back online. Some idiot had cut through the cables. Unfortunately, it took almost the full three days to get through the squabbling of the town leaders. She had had enough of them.

Cassie slapped the back of her hand on the maps spread across the table, then rubbed her temple. "You are the leaders, so lead. There are not enough qualified people in the world to waste on this kind of idiocy. There are bigger problems than some dumb farmer cutting the power cables. Did he die, by the way? If he didn't, then charge him double and set an example of him. This is what your grid maps are for. Make them apply for a map viewing and charge them if they don't use it. Fine them if they hit the cables. I can't be running up here for your incompetence."

"You're too big for your boots." Harry shoved her in the car with a hard pinch to her hip for emphasis.

A truck followed them back.

Bendigo had a sewage blockage. Not enough water flowing through the pipes had caused a backup of the system. A bit more complex than Ballarat, but no squabbling, so she could get the job done and teach others how to troubleshoot in the future.

Two trucks followed them back down the highway.

The inland cities were huge and made Cassie feel claustrophobic. She preferred being on the highway where she could see a long way in all directions, rather than being hemmed in by buildings. She gazed out the window of the car at wide brown fields dotted with kangaroo and longed for the ocean instead.

A pattern emerged over the next few weeks. Specs listed the jobs and accompanied them to negotiate on Bryanth's behalf. Harry would drive her there, dogging her every step. She had to learn to ignore him so she could concentrate on her work. Trying to escape had proven a painful exercise in futility. When the job was done, Harry would drive her back. She never had a chance to shower or change her clothes as Harry would stand in whichever room she was given on a longer stay and make sure she couldn't.

"Boss's orders," was all he would say when she protested. Fighting always left her worse off.

The traders would wrinkle their noses at the stench of her but no one complained. They couldn't risk not having her skills. "Luckily Airport has you to trade; it's way too hard to get anyone qualified from New Melbourne." A twist of pain filled her gut every time New Melbourne was mentioned.

CHAPTER THIRTEEN

The ocean is seldom quiet. It roars and crashes in heavy weather; it ebbs and flows with a gentle susurration on softer days; it pings and pops and bubbles; it sings and protests with hearty slaps against the barriers, but it is rarely quiet.

For someone who lived on the sea, the noise existed as the background to life—like a second heartbeat, barely noticed, intrinsically part of existence.

It was an absence of this sound that itched at Cassie's consciousness.

The car had been still for an hour, windows down, while she slept across the back seat. She had slept through most of the long journey into the high mountain territories. Sleeping helped quell the motion sickness from being in the backseat of an unfamiliar ground vehicle.

Looking up into the canopy of enormous trees made her head spin. The sunlight danced through the leaves and sent shards of brightness into her retinas. She closed her eyes again.

A heady scent of eucalyptus had replaced the familiar salty air her nostrils were used to. It tickled at her sinuses until she sneezed.

A sudden, loud thump against the side of the car made her jump.

"Get out, girly. The boss wants you."

Cassie swung her legs out of the car and pulled her sweaty tee-shirt away from her skin. The humidity in the forest made everything sticky. "Why did Bryanth come instead of Specs?"

"Don't know, don't care. It's up this way."

A series of wooden steps led up the hill from the car park, meandering through the trees in a steady incline. Undergrowth grew thick and thorny less than a metre either side of the track. Cassie followed the huge back of her guard as he lumbered up the steps. The forest wasn't completely silent. A few warbles and chirps could be heard in the distance. Insects chirruped and chittered in the undergrowth—few in the midday heat, but enough that the forest had a low constant buzz to it.

"It's a bit like the ocean." She felt a small smile develop.

"What?" The bellow of Harry's voice silenced the nearby creatures.

Her smile evaporated into the humid air. "Nothing, Hairy. Not. A. Thing."

The muscles tensed across the shoulders of the hulk of a man in front of her. He clenched and unclenched his fists, but was too intent on placing his feet on the steep path to turn around and yell at her in his usual fashion.

"For the thousandth time, it's Harry, not Hairy. I wanna . . ." Cassie could hear him grinding the words through his teeth.

"What? Pull my hair like a toddler, Hairy? You really are too big for that behaviour." She stopped her hand in the act of lifting it to touch her head. Her scalp was always tender lately. Harry had not been allowed to pull her up by the hair since her value had increased, but that didn't stop him hurting her if he could get away with it.

He halted on the path and indicated she should go ahead of him, around the bole of a giant tree. He shoved her in the back as she passed, causing her to stumble, but she kept her footing and walked a little faster to be out of his reach.

A clearing opened up where a small crowd was gathered in front of a wooden cabin with a timber shingled roof. The people all had a tough, wiry look to them; thin, brown, most wearing hats and homespun fabrics. All of them were barefoot. Most of the women, even the teenagers, were in various states of pregnancy.

At the front of the crowd was Bryanth, waving an ornate fan in front of his face. Beside him stood a large woman in hemp jeans and a smock. She had her muscular arms tight across her chest, but leaned well away from Bryanth. The look on her face gave Cassie the impression the woman had a bad taste in her mouth.

The woman turned to Cassie and looked her up and down. She unfolded her meaty arms to point at Cassie's chest. "You bring me a kid? This kid is what you are trading? Do you take me for a fool?"

"I am not trading the girl at all, Dody, not at all. I don't trade in people—that would be disgusting. No, I am trading her skills. She is quite clever, this one, and can have your waste disposal problems sorted in no time."

"I don't want a clever kid. I want someone who knows what they're doing. Stop wasting my time and get off my mountain."

The crowd behind Dody muttered angrily. Bryanth pretended to study his fingernails before announcing, "Young Cassie is from New Melbourne."

The crowd gasped. Dody's face looked as if someone had handed her a giant present with shiny golden bows. "Oh, righty then. Righty. Okay, well that explains it. How long can I have her?"

"I can loan her to you for a few weeks to plan out your system and teach your people what they need to know. I expect you to treat her according to her value."

"Yes, yes, certainly. We will fix up a cabin for her right away. Marcus, on to that, lad."

A young man, who had been staring at Cassie, reluctantly loped away into the forest at Dody's command.

"I will leave her guard with her, of course. I don't need to remind you that we don't require her to be in the family way." Bryanth wrinkled his nose and pursed his lips in disgust.

Dody raised herself to her full considerable height and waved her index finger like a baton. "My women choose to repopulate the Earth. No woman here is ever coerced or forced to bring new life into the world. It is a woman's sacred duty and—"

Bryanth lifted his pale palm in her direction, cutting her off mid-sentence. "Save your philosophy for more receptive ears. She is only on loan and won't be here long enough to fulfil any sacred duties. Now Dody, let's talk terms. I am particularly interested in that little mushroom you have up here."

The two leaders moved into the hut, leaving Cassie and her guard as the focus of the crowd's attention. Some moved closer; Cassie moved a step back, but Harry blocked her retreat and pushed her forward with a nasty chuckle.

"Mama, she stinks." A child of about nine looked up to her heavily pregnant mother. "She should have a wash."

The mother looked embarrassed and smiled at Cassie who was blushing at the comment. "Do you need to freshen up? I'll take you to the washing block. I'm Leslie." The woman waved the crowd away and led Cassie through the trees behind the cabin. Harry followed close at her heels.

"We have plenty of creek water to wash in. Where are your clothes?"

Cassie pulled at the front of her sticky tee-shirt. "This is it. This is all I have. Sorry. Have you got a spare toothbrush? I would kill for a toothbrush."

"I am sure you don't need to go to those extremes. I can find something for you and perhaps a change of clothes until yours are clean. Would that help? Mimi, run and fetch some clothes, a toothbrush, a comb and some paste."

The child ran off to do her mother's bidding.

Cassie felt tears burn in her eyes but refused to let them fall. Any sign of weakness in front of Harry would lead to trouble. "Thank you."

They reached a shack positioned over a rocky creek. The woman held open the door but put a palm up to stop Harry following them inside. "She doesn't need a guard in here. There is only one way in and only me in here with her, now step aside so I can close the door."

Harry actually did as he was asked. Cassie found her whole face forming an 'O' of surprise. Leslie closed the door and wiped one hand down the other in a dismissive gesture.

Inside, the shack was cool and shadowy, the water flowing over the rocks beneath the floor. A small walkway ran between the seats lining the other three walls, and there was a large gap in the centre where the water bubbled into a deep pool. A golden glow of sunlight peeped in under the floorboards, giving an amber hue to the water flowing in and out. The pool became darker than night further down.

"Strip off your things and we can wash them. There are towels on the shelf next to the door."

Cassie pulled off her clothes and heard the woman's sharp intake of breath. She held up her hand to stop the woman asking questions, putting a finger to her lips to indicate they should be quiet, and pointed at the door. "Is there any soap?"

"Next to the towels." The woman had difficulty speaking and sounded as though she was going to be sick. She reached down for the discarded clothes and threw them in a basket, blinking her eyes rapidly at the stench.

"How long have you been wearing these?

"Too long." Cassie eased herself into the pool of water, gasping at the intense cold on her sweaty skin. Goosebumps formed immediately. She slid completely into the water, feeling with her toes for the rocks that lined the pool. Exploring with her hands, she found an outcrop to sit on and she scrubbed, and scrubbed, and scrubbed at her dirty bruised skin.

For the first time in weeks, she could see the results of Harry's unrelenting torment of her. Bruises of every colour from black to sickly yellow dotted her skin. The rapid flow of the water washed away the dirt and scabs. Her hair had not been clean since the swim on Melton Beach, and she imagined she could feel each hair as it separated from where it was glued to the rest with sweat, dirt, food and old mud.

She looked at her body in the limited golden glow of sunlight at the water's edge. She ran a hand over the hard edge of her pelvic bones and onto her slightly concave abdomen; walked her fingers up her rib cage, counting each one and tapped a path across her jutting collarbones. She felt her shoulder and the tender flesh that had emerged from the encrusted mud of a poultice Aunty had put on her so long ago. It looked healthy, which was a good thing, even if the rest of her was malnourished.

A knock at the door made Cassie's heart race and she dropped into the pool until the water came up to her nostrils.

Mimi popped her head in. "Can I come in?"

"Of course, love. Give Cassie what she needs."

"Here y'are." The child handed Cassie a wooden toothbrush and a pot of paste.

Cassie almost moaned in pleasure as she pressed the bristles against her gums. She leaned back and massaged the inside of her mouth, brushing away the accumulated muck her mouth had endured. She rinsed and brushed and rinsed again for a good ten minutes, then ran her tongue around her teeth, feeling the smoothness of the enamel.

"Oh, that feels so good, you can't imagine how good that is." She curled her tongue up under her lip and down the front of her bottom teeth. "Mmm, so good. Thank you, Leslie."

A hefty fist bashed against the side of the hut, startling them all. "Get a move on, the boss wants to talk to you. There's not that much of you to take so long."

Cassie reluctantly climbed out of the pool and reached for the towel Leslie held for her. She rubbed at her skin, wincing at the tender places which numbered higher than the not tender ones.

Leslie handed her some underwear. The bra fitted around her, but was too roomy in the cup. The undies covered more of her than she imagined undies could, but felt comfortable. They all smelled so fresh and clean. The dress—made of a dull, yellow hemp fibre—felt scratchy against her newly clean skin and hung to her mid-shin like a sack.

"Probably better if you don't look interesting." Leslie smiled and helped dry Cassie's hair which had grown out of her preferred pixie cut almost to her shoulders. "I'll tie this in short braids for you, to keep it out of your way when you work."

Another hefty thump against the door. Cassie clenched her fists in her lap and clamped her teeth together. Leslie patted her shoulder. Mimi looked frightened and clung to her mother.

"Hurry up. Five minutes or I'm coming in to get you."

The heat hit them as they emerged from the washing hut, but the hemp was a cooler material than the tee-shirt. Mimi carried the basket of washed clothes towards a line set up between some trees and began to peg them up. Leslie stayed beside Cassie as they returned to the first clearing.

"Hmmm. Oh my, I forgot you were a girl. Wait, did I even know you were a girl?" Bryanth giggled behind his fan. "Does it matter? Look at you in your hempy homespun with your shiny brown hair. You would fit right in here amongst the . . . er . . . locals."

Bryanth tapped his index fingers against his thumbs in a rapid motion before pointing both index fingers at her. "But you are only staying for two weeks, my little treasure. Dody will fill you in on what they expect from you. Harry will not leave your side, for your own protection of course. Right then, I'm off."

***

Cassie surveyed the backs of the people digging the future wetlands. She wiped the sweat from her forehead with her forearm, keeping her muddy hands away from her face.

"Dody, if they don't get the levels right at this point, the whole thing will be more trouble than not. An effective drainage system has to be able to self-clean, and an effective filtration area needs to keep the water clean for food growth in your fields. I have drawn you designs for the dry toilets and the wetlands for purifying grey water from your village, but getting the angle right at the top end ensures it will all pass freely through the system into the main wetland. You can't just do it by halves. It's critical we get it right. I doubt I will be able to come back later to fix it, so let's not need to fix it."

"You're quite the little boss when you are running the show. All right, then, we'll get the angles right. The toilets will be finished before you go. What else do we need to know?"

The sun tangled in the branches of the trees in a heavy golden ball when Dody called it a day with a hefty bellow. "Come on everyone, food is on the tables. Tools down, wash up. Let's go."

People downed tools and headed for the shallow pool outside the wash hut to clean up before sharing a meal. The stream of people broke around the rock of Harry and came together directly past him.

"Come on lass, walk with me." Dody put a heavy arm across Cassie's shoulders and walked her to the wash pond. "Why did you leave New Melbourne? That is the place we all dream of going to someday. And how in hell did you end up in that repulsive man's grip?"

"Stupidity, Dody. I made a bad decision for the wrong reasons and . . ." Cassie shrugged.

"We all do that. Is it true that everyone has a university degree there?" Dody's eyes shone with a longing Cassie could barely understand.

"Everyone is educated and most of us get degrees when we are of an age. The population is wide from a few pre-Rise elderly to tiny babies, just like here. We value education and science. I've got an environmental engineering degree. My parents insisted, and right now I think that is what has kept me alive."

"Do you really only eat seaweed out there?"

Cassie laughed and a moment later Dody laughed with her. "Of course not, we grow all sorts of food in multi-storey hydroponic barges, and aqua harvest. We trade a lot of plant based protein with the floating cities and the mainland—it's our biggest commodity. Probably eighty per cent of what we produce is traded. We usually trade for plastics from landfill and recycle the plastics into everything you can imagine, and trade that back as our second-biggest product. I love plastic, don't you?"

"Not really. It is hardy stuff but I think of it as a symbol of the fall of mankind."

"Ah, okay. I guess you could look at it like that, but we recycle it into useful things. Most of the modern roads in the cities are made from it, did you know?"

"Yes, but did *you* know Marcus has taken a shine to you?" Dody asked with a cheeky grin. "If you wanted, we could arrange something. We don't hold with men owning a woman, but we encourage pairings if both parties are keen."

Cassie looked at Marcus, busy carrying something, somewhere. He could be the way to escape Bryanth, but then what? Pregnant, stuck in the mountains, never see the sea? She shook her head. "No, that's okay, Dody. I don't think I have time for all that. He is nice to look at though."

"Suit yourself." Dody patted her on the shoulder with a laugh and moved in a way that blocked Harry dogging Cassie's heels. It had been the same since she arrived, someone would walk with her or behind her or call out to her whenever she might be alone with Harry, escorting her to her cabin each night and meeting her in the morning to escort her to breakfast. She had resented it at first until she realised what they were doing; protecting her from him.

Leslie met her on the path and hooked an arm in hers. Mimi skipped along the path behind them.

"You must be hungry after all that work."

"You've been working hard, too. How can any of you cook in this heat when you're pregnant?"

The two women chatted all the way back to the dining hall. Mimi hugged them both and skipped off to sit with her friends.

Cassie loved this shared eating with chatter and laughter filling the air—it reminded her of team lunches.

Everyone grabbed platters of food and shared them around. Talk flowed like a river and Cassie relaxed into the camaraderie, answering the same questions she had been answering for the past week-and-a-half like: How do the wetlands work? What happens without a good waste management system? How much water will dry toilets save?

". . . the water is filtered as it passes through the leaf litter and plant stems and interacts with the roots and soil in the wetland basin . . . diseases, viruses, parasites, can all be avoided if the . . . heaps . . ."

"No work talk at the table. Let the girl have a rest," Dody boomed at her people—and they really were her people, as if she were the mother of them all. They looked to her for guidance, comfort, leadership and advice, and accepted her direction and discipline.

"I like it here, Leslie." Cassie leaned toward Leslie.

"Maybe you should stay. I'm sure Dody can arrange something."

"Maybe you should shut up," an ugly voice interrupted them. "She gets the job done, then we leave. No discussion."

Cassie flinched at the quiet snarl of Harry's voice behind her.

"Don't speak to me like that." Leslie stood up and raised her voice.

"Don't speak to any of my people like that." The threat in Dody's voice was clear. She had appeared quietly behind Leslie and moved her to one side. Eye-to-eye, she equalled Harry in height and muscle.

She leaned forward, her nose almost touching his. "If Cassie tells me she wants to stay, she would be most welcome and there would be nothing you could do about it. You are merely tolerated in these mountains—you are not a guest, and the law here is mine. Don't overstretch my tolerance."

Harry grabbed Cassie firmly by her wounded shoulder and dug in his fingertips. Cassie cried out in pain, but he kept a firm grip on her. He made a cutting sweep with his free hand. "She goes back; she belongs to my boss. No discussion."

"Belongs, does she? Cassie?"

"Dody, it's okay, I can't stay anyway. We're almost finished what I can do here. Don't worry, I'm okay. Let's just eat, I'm famished." Cassie didn't try to free herself from his grip, but after a few moments, Harry released her. She sat in her seat and pretended to eat. No one was fooled.

CHAPTER FOURTEEN

The car ride was long, down the mountains and back to the airport beaches. It gave Cassie time to think. The two weeks in the mountains had flown by. She'd left clutching a bundle of clothes, a toothbrush and comb, and her very own towel—gifts from her new friends. She didn't know what the trade had been for her skills, but she knew that Bryanth was reaping the rewards.

As soon as they arrived back from the mountains, Specs scurried to the car and spoke quietly with Harry.

Her new braids made it difficult for Harry to twist his fingers in, so he grabbed the end of a short braid and dragged her along to a tent at the rear of the one Bryanth held his audiences in. This tent was small and a mesh wall joined the two. Harry clamped his hand over her mouth and held her firmly pressed against his chest with the other.

Cassie could see into the bigger tent where Glen stood in front of Bryanth who sat on his gilded chair.

Bryanth clicked his fingers and the bespectacled man stepped forward and offered a bundle of clothing to Glen.

"There you go. Hmmm? I told you I would return the clothing when she earned her own."

"I said these were hers now. Where is she?" Glen held the bundle out as if he would return them, but Specs stepped back.

"Not that it's any of your business, but I sent her up into the mountains on a trade deal. Technically, she didn't earn her new clothes. The mountain people gave her some good old home-spun hemp—neck-to-ankle coverage as is right and proper. She did look quite the part and those mountain men noticed. A bit of new blood up there would prove beneficial, don't you think?"

"What have you done?" Glen stepped toward Bryanth. Harry tensed but held Cassie still.

"Me? Done? Hmmm? Glen, the histrionics. Goodness, are you having a little breakdown? You wanted her cleaned up, she's cleaned up. Fresh clothes, clean hair—quite a pleasant chestnut in the sun, by the way—and I think she actually made some friends. Dody was quite taken with her."

Bryanth picked at his left index cuticle with his well-manicured right thumb.

"You really are becoming a bore, Glen. You have had three refusals now and I am not usually so tolerant. I simply cannot be bothered with a bloodbath this week, my schedule is so full. I am sure your people will appreciate that. Don't come back now. Run along." He turned away.

Glen clenched his fists around the bundle of clothing, turned on his heel, and left the tent.

Harry leaned his mouth close to Cassie's ear. "Your boyfriend is fucked if he comes back."

Cassie squirmed, forced her mouth open, and bit Harry.

He yelled, letting her go to shake his finger.

"He's not my boyfriend, Hairy, and keep your paws off me."

Harry raised a fist to punch her, but stopped at Bryanth's voice.

"Bring her in."

He pinched the soft underside of her arm instead, before dragging her around the tent by the braid.

"Why the hell does your goon always hurt me?" Cassie pulled her hair free of Harry's thick fist.

"My, my. You are feisty today, hmmm. Could it be

our recent visitor has got your blood up? How delightful. Harry resents having to babysit . . . how did he put it . . . 'a worthless stinkin' little bitch'. That's what you said, Harry?"

"Yeah, boss."

"Harry has no real concept of how far from worthless you are to me, but he is jealous because he would much prefer to be my bodyguard than yours."

"Bodyguard? I'm covered in bruises from the brute."

"You really are a naive little thing. Is there no danger to young ladies out there in utopia? Harry is . . . how shall I put this . . . more inclined to hurt things than hug them. He is on strict instructions to limit the level of hurt he inflicts on you, since I want you functioning at peak efficiency and that won't happen if any of my other men decide you needed . . . er . . . hugging. Or if I order Harry to take the gloves off. Am I making myself clear?"

The blood drained from Cassie's face and her stomach hurt. She gulped, and her voice came out barely above a whisper. "Abundantly."

"Good. Let me tell you a funny story, hmmm? I'm feeling so buoyant, I do enjoy messing with dear Glen. It's my fault he was kicked off New Melbourne you see . . ."

Glen was in New Melbourne?

"His life-long dream shattered by little me before he could learn a thing. You don't need the messy details, but suffice it to say, he resents me for it, and we have been rivals ever since. He does have that noble streak about him, so normally I can't get under his skin, but something about you keeps pulling him over here, and that makes you the perfect weapon. It's a pity Dody cleaned you up, filthy you was really upsetting him. That game has played out so you can stay clean now. You were disgusting to be around."

Bryanth gave a melodramatic sigh and turned away.

"Where are we sending her next?"

CHAPTER FIFTEEN

"Glen?"

He stared at the woman in front of him. She was much thinner than last time he had seen her, greyer hair, but still mostly long and black. Her skin was far more weathered—natural of course after fifteen years—but he recognised her instantly.

She barely stood level with his mid-chest but seemed taller somehow. A face, devoid of emotion, was belied by the slight tremor and whitened knuckles gripping the tablet in one hand.

"Mrs Orm." He stood stiffly in front of her.

"Why didn't you come back to my classes? You started with such promise and then foof, gone."

"I got the message loud and clear: You don't waste

resources on one damned fool, Mrs Orm. I, being that fool, had to leave."

She pulled her face back from him and looked puzzled in a very familiar way. "How silly. Really? You didn't take that to heart, did you? We tell that to all the students. It is supposed to convince them to knuckle into their studies, getting their heads down after perfectly normal youthful shenanigans. I can't believe you took it to heart. I was sorry we lost you. Now, what brings you back?"

Glen felt like someone had sucked all the air from his lungs. He sat abruptly on the chair he had stood up from when Mrs Orm had entered the interview room. He tried to breathe but nothing happened. It seemed an eternity before his lungs remembered what they were supposed to do and acknowledged his gasping. "All these years. I wasted all these years."

"I'm very sorry, Glen, I don't have much time for your little crisis. Could you please explain your business and we shall see if we can assist. It states here you have applied several times for engineering assistance, is that why you are here?" She tapped her small screen a few times, chewing her lip.

"No, it's about a girl from here. She needs help. You might know her, she's called Cassie . . ."

"Cassie?" All of a sudden, she was in his face,

grabbing his shirt sleeve. "What does she look like, what do you know about her? Is she all right?"

Glen tried to pull back from her, but she twisted the front of his shirt in her little fists. He held his hands away from her.

"Tell me." Now her face was all emotion, her eyes glassy and stormy full. "Tell me about Cassie!"

"She washed up in a storm about six weeks ago. Early twenties, light brown hair, hazel eyes. She was hit by lightning."

Mrs Orm slapped her hand over her mouth. An animal groan escaped around her fingers. "Rodger!" She screamed the name and ran from the room. "Rodger!"

Within moments, the room filled with official-looking people bombarding him with questions. It took some time, but finally they understood how Cassie had arrived among his people and how she had been captured by the rival gang of Combers. He told them what he knew of how she was being treated and that he believed the Airport gang had traded her to the high mountain people.

"Traded!?" The shriek cut through all the noise. "How can they trade my daughter? It's barbaric!" Mrs Orm threw herself into the arms of her husband and sobbed into his chest.

"Your daughter?" Glen looked at the couple in the doorway.

"If only we'd been here earlier. We were going to surprise her . . . We should have sent an email. I knew we should have come back sooner. I never meant to leave her alone so much. Oh Rodger, what have we done? What have we done?" Her sobs muffled as he wrapped his arms tight around her.

The older man's face was just as tormented as his wife's. "Come, dear, they will sort it out. It is all a mistake. There, there, dear, come and we'll find a nice cup of tea and let these people do their job. There, there."

The man's quiet calm voice seemed to soothe the distress in his wife and he guided her from the room.

"You're really going to help her?" Glen looked up at Old Mark.

"Of course we'll help her, lad, she's one of our own. We've been searching for weeks and she is *their* daughter." He indicated the Orms. "They came home to surprise her for her birthday, but she was missing. They'll turn the planet on its head to get her back. We've a good trade deal with the mountains, it shouldn't be too messy."

CHAPTER SIXTEEN

"Mildura Sea is named for the city sunk beneath the waters . . ." Specs droned on like a human encyclopedia.

The bespectacled man was travelling with Cassie and Harry to negotiate the latest contract.

"It has an enormous coastline, but only two cities—Broken Hill on the west coast, and Echuca on the east—with 650 kilometres between them. Both cities have built up a good shipping trade and the Combers on both sides are fierce rivals. The cities have their own police forces who have a fragile working relationship with their Combers, but they do not tolerate other Combers in either city. There could also be issues with the Echuca Combers if they find out we are in town. They may see us as encroaching on their turf. Avoid the beaches."

"Do you have a name?" Cassie asked without turning to look at him.

"Not one you need to be aware of." Specs changed the page on his screen. "We'll be there soon." He pushed his glasses up his nose and continued to read, making notes with the stylus every few lines.

"I'll keep calling you Specs in my head, then."

"As good a name as any, I suppose." He pushed his glasses back up his nose again.

"What's the job?" Cassie had her elbow on the window, her hand playing with the wind.

"I believe it will be water purification. Perhaps some pollution control as well, and checking faults in their systems. The systems shut down about a decade ago."

Cassie sighed and lay her head on her arm, letting the hot wind twist knots through her hair. "This is not what I was trained to do." She watched the trees sitting on the horizon, never coming closer, birds circling high in the sky, broken buildings crumbling to nothing, long yellow stands of grass as far as the eye could see.

"Oh?" The little man put down his pen, closed his book, and looked at her encouragingly.

She continued to stare out at the empty country and dip her fingers through the air pressure. "These jobs are maintenance crew work. My degree set me up to be a planner. I'm supposed to look at the big picture and come up with concepts and ideas and plan the infrastructure that will make life better for whole communities. Instead, I'm up to my neck in sewage half the time, rewiring fuse boxes any teenager in New Melbourne could fix. Or—more kids work—polishing muck off solar panels, supervising toilet digging crews; doing the jobs of sparkies and plumbers. Talk about a waste of my pote—" She clamped her lips over the words of Old Mark slipping out of her mouth.

"Perhaps my employer needs to rethink how he trades your skills."

Cassie swung around to look at him. "Even maintenance jobs should have earned my freedom over and over by now. He can't keep holding me captive. It isn't right."

"Shut your mouth, bitch. You'll stay until my boss says you leave." Harry turned from the driver's seat to look at her, dragging the steering wheel with him. They swerved onto the gravel.

Cassie screamed. Specs clutched the notebook to his chest, with the other hand twisted around his seat belt. Harry pulled them back onto the smoother plastic road. They relaxed but did not resume talking for the rest of the journey.

CHAPTER SEVENTEEN

"You can't just chase around the countryside after a girl, you have duties and responsibilities here." Rabbit crossed her arms and scowled.

"She wasn't in the mountains." Glen thumped one fist into the palm of his other hand. "New Melbourne said they didn't need my interference, but I let her down. She was under my—"

"Yes, we know, but you can't keep beating yourself up for what that mongrel over at Airport had his people do. He likes messing with people's heads and you fell right into it."

"You have to take care of your own, Glen," Rob said, scowling. "Us. We need you focused, we have a winter to prepare for." Rob emphasised his words by jabbing the table with a thick forefinger.

"You need to speak with Melton City Council and keep them and their police out of our business. The beaches are ours. Also, we have trade negotiations organised up in Echuca and you are going. That's final." Gumpy looked around and everyone nodded.

"We would never have landed the trade without Cassie's diving gear." Andy was new to the leadership crew and swallowed rapidly, his Adam's apple bobbing up and down as several people thumped or shushed him. "It paid off better than we could have imagined, so let's make this a tribute to her."

Glen punched the table, making mugs and cups rattle and jump. "Tribute, my rear end. She's not bloody dead!" He raked his fingers through his hair. "All right. All right. I'll go. But after the trade deal, I'm going to find her and help her get home. We owe her that. Now tell me about Echuca."

CHAPTER EIGHTEEN

Cassie sat quietly at the long, polished wooden table. The people around the table were arguing with Specs. Voices rose and fell as negotiations floundered.

This! This is my chance. Harry's outside. I can make this work.

"There is nothing else to discuss. We don't want her." The spokesperson for the Echuca council stood up to emphasise the decision.

Specs leaned back in his chair and pushed his glasses up, looking worried.

The man to his left pointed at Cassie, sitting silently at the end of the table. "We were expecting a qualified engineer from New Melbourne, not this little mountain girl."

Cassie smoothed the homespun dress across her knees. Her hair was in messy braids she had tried to teach herself to do, but could never keep tidy with Harry's regular incursions. She twirled a braid around her finger.

"She is a qualified engineer from New Melbourne. We have extensive testimonials on her work."

The entire table of counsellors turned to look directly at her. "Are you, girl?" a grandfatherly man asked her kindly.

Cassie made her voice sound small and young and widened her eyes as she looked at each person and waited long seconds before answering. "Am I what, sir?"

"An engineer from New Melbourne?"

"Well Sir, I'm quite clever, sir, Dody said so. I helped organise the purification marsh and the dry toilets, sir. It's so beautiful in the trees up there, you should visit. You have to get the angle just right on the slopes, for the flow. I love to read technical books, sir." She smiled at him as sweetly as she could.

The whole committee turned to Specs and poured their outrage at him.

"Dody? Is that the matriarch from Marysville?"

"This girl looks about, what . . . seventeen . . . eighteen, perhaps? Hardly scientist material, even if she is self-proclaimed clever."

"How dare you try to con us. We shall have this

investigated.”

"Get out of this chamber at once and take the girl with you.”

"We'll have to make contact with New Melbourne. This debacle is going to put us way behind schedule.”

"Have them escorted from the building.”

Specs was visibly shaking. Grabbing Cassie by the upper arm, he dragged her towards the door. "What have you done? Why now? You need to work with me on this.” He did not raise his voice but each word burst from him on a spray of spittle.

Cassie dug her heels into the carpet.

"What are you doing?” Specs hissed at her through his teeth. "They made it clear we are to leave. Move.”

"Let go of me.” Cassie raised her voice and pulled back. She put all the fear and pain of the past few weeks into the statement.

The committee members looked up.

"Here, let that girl go. If she tells you to let go, then let go. We won't tolerate that sort of thing.”

Specs dropped his hold on her arm and stepped away.

"Are you all right, dear girl?”

Cassie shook her head, her mouth pulled down to match the sad wrinkling of her forehead.

The motherly woman asking the question put an

arm around her and led her back to the table. "Simon, call the police."

Specs bit his lip, took a last look at Cassie, and scurried from the room.

Harry bellowed from outside the chamber. She could hear him arguing with Specs and then the council chamber doors shuddered under the onslaught of his fists.

"I'll get you, bitch. I'll get you. Bryanth isn't here to stop me."

The yelling cut off, replaced by the sounds of heavy thumps as he was herded from the building by security.

Cassie didn't have to feign the fear on her face.

CHAPTER NINETEEN

The bell chimed over the door as Glen stepped through. He smiled at the shiny, well-polished brass, a far cry from the dull thing it had been when he brought it here.

"Hey, Giani?" he called into the murky depths of the swap shop. Something fell heavily, followed by a colourful bout of profanities.

"Can't understand a word of that, mate," Glen yelled down a narrow passage through piles of boxes.

A bent man hobbled along the passage and squinted up from under a thick, bushy uni-brow. He ducked under the counter and embraced the much taller man. "My goodness gracious. Glen, such a long time, my friend. What brings you up here to my beautiful city? Elisa will be so happy to feed you." He patted Glen's abdomen. "Where are you staying? With us of course, I won't hear another word about it."

"Would I dare refuse?"

"Is good. Come, come, in the back. The grandchildren are here, they will love to see you, too. Elisa, guess who's here."

Glen squeezed under the counter and along the passageway, following Giani to a brightly lit doorway at the far end.

Elisa immediately embraced him with a squeal of delight, pushed him into a chair and started piling food in front of him.

Giani set two small glasses on the table and poured some of his infamous wine into them. "Salute. Cin, cin." The glasses clinked and they both swallowed the fiery liquid in one gulp.

"Now, you tell me why you . . ." The doorbell tinkled. "I be right back, I go see who it is. Eat, eat."

Elisa handed Glen a mug of her precious tea and sat opposite him. "It's so good to see you. Are you staying long?"

The children ran in from the living room and leaned on their Aunt to stare at Glen.

"They don't remember you, it's been too long. You must be so busy these days."

"They're so big, I remember them crawling around

their mother's feet. Hey, kids." The kids ran back to the living room with exclamations of boredom. The adults smiled indulgently. "Busier than I ever imagined, Elisa. What is keeping you out of mischief these days?"

"Dad, of course. Since Mum died, I spend most of my time looking after him or the kids. Maria is working at the hospital now that she is qualified, so I have the kids for her. I still study—" She held a finger to her mouth, then signed for him to stand up.

A blue globe flashed a rapid series of on-and-off light above the door. She tiptoed into the living room and signalled the kids to be silent and follow her, opened up a hidden room in a wall behind a stack of boxes, and ushered them all inside.

C-o-m-b-e-r-s, she finger-spelled. She flicked her index fingers up and towards her. *Danger.*

Glen ran the thumb of a gun shape down his chest. *Why?*

Elisa tapped the thumb of a fist to her temple, then moved an okay sign away from her body. *Know not.* She shrugged. She pointed to her middle finger, *i,* and tapped her index and middle finger together on the same fingers of her other hand, *f*—spelling *if*—and followed it by two more f's for *father.* Then she made the *c* shape and shook it in front of her forehead, *worried.* She crossed her arms and pointed to her opposite shoulders, opened her hands to point forward, *we*, then she slid her flat hand down the underside of her arm to her elbow, *hide*.

They settled to wait, each hugging a child.

Twenty minutes passed.

"Come out, my loves, all is well." They could hear Giani moving the wall and the fake pile of boxes. His smiling face peeped in and he reached for a grandchild. "Come, loves—my worry is past. Where is that chocolate cake you made, Elisa? The children should eat in the living room as a treat, yes?"

"Now we can talk." The men sat at the table. "Local Combers with two not from around here. Not usual, it not so normal that they work together. The outsiders lose something, ask locals for help, they bring them here. They know Giani knows where to find things. I did not like the look of them, I no like to help with this one, maybe." Giani tapped the table. "Some things I not like to find. I keep my family safe."

"I know better than to ask, even though I'm curious. Great job with the Morse code on the light by the way. The kids were really good."

Giani beamed his pride.

"So the locals are dangerous, what is the local law like?"

"The police are only as good as the city that trains them and the laws they make, not like the old days when the police were nationwide and we had one law for all. The Combers here are not like you—no real Combers, not pick up gifts from the sea. They work with the docks; they have power but no integrity. The police maybe have integrity but not much power and me, Giani, I find things."

He rubbed his chin and looked worried. A moment later he slapped the table making all the glasses jump.

"I not help with this one. Let's talk about you trade. What you got?"

CHAPTER TWENTY

"You say they kidnapped you from a beach? Is that correct?" The police officer typed one finger at a time on a tiny notepad.

"Yes." Cassie switched between chewing her fingernails and peeling the ends off.

The officer looked up, then returned to typing each letter with excruciating slowness. "And you say they prevented you from leaving, using violence and coercion? Is that correct?"

"Yes." Frustration made Cassie snap the word out.

"Miss, I am trying to assist you, there is no need for that attitude. Now you say they were forcing you to do your work as a trade for goods, but you never saw any of these goods, do I have that right?"

"You have asked me all these questions and I have answered them, are you actually going to help me or not?"

"We need to ascertain all the details before we can proceed, Miss. Were any of these people related to you or in an intimate relationship with you?"

"No!" The word scraped through her gritted teeth. "I never met them, I didn't know them, they stuck a bag over my head and dropped me on a floor. How is this helping me right now? There is a thug out there in your city who has threatened to 'get me'—and I know from bitter experience just how violent he can be—and you don't seem to be doing anything about it. What do I have to do to get some actual help?"

"Start by calming down, Miss. I suppose you can't have upset them in an outfit like that . . ."

"What the hell? I cannot believe I am hearing this. I really was naive to think the world would be just like home. I'm an idiot. Look, forget it, just tell me where I can find somewhere to stay with nothing to trade but my bare hands?"

The police officer sat with fingers hovering above the keyboard. "I'm afraid I can't do that, Miss. The council wants me to investigate who you are and why you and your friends attempted to fraudulently obtain council funds on the pretence that you are some kind of qualified person from New Melbourne. You claim you are a victim, but so far you haven't told me anything to corroborate your story. Let's start with the basics. What is your name?"

"Cassie Orm, and they are not my friends."

"Like the Orm scientists who just cleaned up the parasite infestation in the remains of the Daintree Rainforest? Those Orms?"

"Yes. They're my parents."

"Sure, and I can touch type. What is your name, really?"

Cassie dropped her head forward and pulled her own hair with both hands. "This is a nightmare."

The officer stood up and indicated she should do the same. "Hold your wrists up please, Miss."

"Why are you putting me in cuffs? I haven't done anything wrong."

He clicked the cuffs closed over her wrists. "It's just a precaution, Miss. We are walking to the police station for further questioning. It is only a six-minute stroll but I need to ensure you will not do something foolish in those six minutes. Come along."

He tugged her forward with a finger hooked around the link of the cuffs. She stumbled, but he grabbed her forearm and prevented her fall.

"No need for histrionics, Miss. It's just a short

walk."

Several enormous trees overshadowed the two-storey edifice of the council office. Cassie had never seen trees so big. Solar absorbers hung from every branch, flashing in the sunlight. If she hadn't been so distressed, she might have enjoyed the walk, but all she noticed was a lawn so ancient it sat almost a hand-span above the footpath she dragged her feet along.

Traffic passed them; mostly bicycles, barrows, wagons and rickshaws. One solar-electric personal vehicle whizzed past. The majority of people were on foot; a few cast curious glances her way, then pretended not to have seen anything.

She leaned back as far as her captured hands would allow and looked up through the dappled light of the tree canopy at the clear blue sky above. An abundance of birds whistled and warbled amongst the leaves, and somewhere in a nearby pond, a throaty amphibian called.

The police officer clicked his tongue in exasperation.

Without warning, two huge arms wrapped around Cassie's upper torso and lifted her into the air. The officer stumbled as the cuffs were dragged from his fingers.

"No!" Cassie's scream caught the attention of everyone in the street. The birds fell silent.

"Release her at once." The officer attempted to

pull his baton from the belt clip.

Harry released one meaty arm from around Cassie—swinging her into the iron grip of the other, squeezing air from her lungs—and punched the officer full in the face.

Blood spurted from his broken nose. It took less than the fall of an eyelash for people to sense danger and scatter, leaving an empty street.

Cassie kicked and squirmed, trying to break free.

Harry swung his hand and planted a hot stinging slap to her entire face. He grabbed her chin, almost crushing her jaw. His hot breath on her cheek, he snarled in her ear. "Gotcha now, bitch. Let's go play punching bags. I'll do all the punching."

"Pud der down ad onsth."

Harry looked down at the blood coated police officer and sneered. "Make me, dick head."

"I cawd for bagup."

Cassie felt an infinitesimal loosening of the arm around her, gathered all her focus into her legs, and kicked Harry as hard as she could with her heels to his thighs. She connected with an area less muscular, and—with a roar—he dropped her to the concrete path.

She pushed herself up and limped a few steps. *Move Cassie, move.*

Without looking back, she ran. Cuffed hands made

running ungainly and awkward, but years of jogging around the city perimeter and a lighter gait gave her an advantage over Harry's solid bulk.

She sprinted down tree-lined streets, past shops and cafés, and people who leaped out of her way—or perhaps not out of *her* way so much, as her deadly pursuer's. He had a dogged stamina and Cassie soon found her lead diminishing.

Hair stood up on the back of her neck, and she didn't know if she was imagining his heavy breath behind her or not, but she could not spare the seconds to turn and look. Leg muscles hot, her sides aching, her breathing adrenaline-fuelled, heart thumping in fear, she ducked down side streets looking for somewhere safe to hide.

Get into a shop, lots of people. No, that won't stop him.

Her headlong flight halted brutally as her hair became tangled in his fingers.

"You won't get away this time."

He panted, struggling to slow his breathing. She took a small insane second of pleasure knowing she had made him work hard to catch her.

He lifted her by the hair and gripped the handcuffs, pulling her arms up, and threw her on the ground. The impact sent shock waves along her spine. All the air escaped her lungs. Her hands felt like they were being severed. Then a boot hit her thigh.

This isn't happening, it isn't happening, stop, stop, stop, stop, stop . . .

It did stop, eventually, but it took a few minutes for her to realise. She rolled away from the place of pain, her brain in survival mode only. She watched a tangled mess of arms and legs where Harry ought to be, but could not make sense of it. She stood up painfully, slowly, and limped away. She thought she heard someone call to her and tried to move faster.

She found a corner and another and another and then Specs stepped in front of her. "Cassie, stop."

She stepped around him and limped on.

"Cassie, you have to come with me."

She began to run.

"Cassie, it's not what you think. I won't hurt you. Come back."

Somehow she found reserves to break into a sprint, but the reserves could not last, and she fell into a small alleyway behind a building with a large rubbish bin. She squeezed in behind it. Some animal made a moaning sound, but when she bumped her bruised thigh and the moan grew louder she knew it was herself.

CHAPTER TWENTY-ONE

"I have to pick up the kids for Maria, so I'll leave you here, Glen. Dad said you'll get the best deal here for your goods."

Glen and Elisa stood outside an old brick building not far from the docks. "Thanks, E, I'll meet you back at your Dad's."

Inside, the building was cool and shadowy, the deep casement windows keeping out the heat and a lot of light. The place was a busy hive of activity. Other people were haggling prices so Glen waited, admiring merchandise and the old architecture.

". . . Comber trouble in the main street. It was a mess."

Glen pretended he wasn't listening to a new group

who walked in off the street.

". . . police tackled some hulk of a man, a Comber, for attacking one of theirs. The local Combers are saying they don't know him."

"They said the monster was chasing some slip of a girl but she disappeared. Apparently, she was one of those cult kids from the back woods. Man, could she run. Even after he . . ."

They moved into another room. Something about the conversation niggled at Glen.

"What can I help you with?"

Trade began.

CHAPTER TWENTY-TWO

The noise came again. Elisa wiped her hands on the dishtowel and listened intently. There it was.

"It sounds like a hurt animal, Aunty E."

"Stay here kids, I'll take a look." Elisa picked up the broom and carefully opened the door into the alley behind the shop.

Slowly, very slowly she approached the rubbish bin where the noise was coming from. Broom held high, she bent and peered into the gap between the back of the bin and the wall.

The broom fell to the ground, unheeded. Elisa pressed her back to the bin, her legs on the wall, and pushed with all her might. The bin moved, mere centimetres, but enough to get into the space. A pair of wide, terrified eyes in a dirty, bruised and tear-streaked face looked up at her. Blood crusted the girl's yellow fibre dress at the sleeves and knees.

"Hell, what happened to you, girl? Come on. Come on." Elisa held out her hand, palm up.

The girl pushed away from her, but let out a yelp of pain. Her whimpering turned into muffled words. "He'll find me. He'll find me. I have to hide."

Elisa noticed the girl wore handcuffs, also covered in blood. "It's okay, love, I have somewhere you can hide. Come on. You can't stay out here in the filth. You'll be safe with me. Come on. It's okay." Elisa kept up a steady croon and reached into the space. "Come on, let's get you cleaned up. Oh you poor thing, come on."

Elisa gently cradled the younger woman under her shoulders. "Come on, come on, let's get you inside."

They negotiated the steps, each footfall punctuated by a little moan of pain.

"Get her some water."

The older child raced to comply, filling a plastic tumbler from the filter jug. Elisa led the girl into the living room and helped her sit in a big armchair. Handing the cup to the girl, she gripped it with shaking hands, spilling some water and making the dry blood ooze down her thin wrists. She sipped through swollen lips, tears sliding silently down her cheeks to join the water in the tumbler.

Elisa knelt on the floor beside her. "I have some fresh clothes and we have enough water for a small bath. It's not much, but I save up so the kids can bathe each week. Would you like that?"

A plethora of emotions ran across the girls face, then she nodded.

"I might even have a pair of shoes. The ones you're wearing have seen better days."

Elisa pottered about finding things, sending the kids to various shelves in their granddad's store, carting buckets into and out of the room, keeping up a constant stream of chatter, hoping it would help the girl feel safe.

"The city should have running water, but we can't get an engineer up to fix it. There are so few qualified people these days, so we have to go to the river and fetch it but we always have clashes with the Combers or others who think they can control all the water. Papa says it will get better, but it is so ridiculous right now. If we had running water again they couldn't bully us at the river. We are okay though, I should be grateful, we have more water than many places—at least we have the rivers. I wish someone would come up from New Melbourne and teach us how to maintain the plumbing, I'm tired of burying our night soil in the communal gardens, well, the fallow fields. Anyway, here you are. I hope you don't mind a more colourful dress. I tried for clothes you could tie on your shoulders because of, er . . . them." Elisa nodded at the cuffs as she handed the girl a bright floral piece of material, a soft towel, some underwear and a pair of shoes.

She pointed to a door.

"The bathroom is that way. Let's get you cleaned up."

They moved slowly together, allowing for the limping gait of the girl.

"I'll have to cut this dress off, there is no other way to get past your bracelets." Elisa produced her sewing scissors and waited.

The girl nodded and Elisa cut the seams across the top and down the length of the sleeves. The pile of yellow hemp slid down the girl, revealing a wrinkled scar covering one shoulder and part of her back, scabs and bruises both new and fading, bleeding abrasions on her elbows, knees, and thighs, raw cuts around her wrists, and bones too close to the skin.

The girl stepped into the shallow water in the bath. She shivered and gasped but lowered herself to a sit.

"Would you like me to wash your hair?"

Elisa watched the girl shake with silent sobs and gently began to pour water onto her tangled hair.

"I wish I could heat it for you, but we haven't got fuel to waste on heating water. Papa says we're going to get solar hot water as soon as we can, and he is looking for some solar window panes. They are hard to get, but if anyone can get some, Papa can. The soap might sting a bit, sorry. I made it myself. I like to put wildflowers in the mixture. It looks pretty, even if it makes no difference to how clean you get."

The whole time she chatted, Elisa soaped the girl's hair and then helped to clean where cuffed hands could not reach. The water became murky as the layers of grime on the girl's skin sluiced into the water.

"I'll fetch another bucket of water and rinse you off. I'll be a few minutes, okay?"

Elisa ran to the kitchen, dabbed her eyes, and lit the little burner under the kettle. She leaned both hands on the bench and sniffed a few *don't cry breaths* up her nose.

She half-filled the bucket with cold water and poured the heated water into it. "I can just go without a cup of tea tonight."

"Is the lady a criminal, Aunty E?"

Elisa smiled at her nephew and niece and shook her head. "No loves, she got Comber trouble."

That explanation was enough. They both nodded and returned to reading their books.

The girl knelt shivering in the filthy bath water—she was reaching for the plug.

"Don't let the water out, we need it for the garden."

The girl pulled her hand back.

"Stand up and I'll rinse you off."

The warmer water came as a pleasurable shock as Elisa slowly poured it out.

"Like Venus rising from the sea," Elisa quipped, as she helped the girl step from the bath.

The girl looked down at her hips and legs, shook her head, and sniffed out a tiny puff of humour. "Botticelli didn't paint stick figures."

The both laughed—short, sharp bursts of relief that quickly ended.

A few minutes later, both young women came out of the bathroom. Elisa opened the safe room.

"I've made up a bed so you can sleep. Stay in here until I come to get you. Don't leave for any reason. There is a night pot back there and I have a litre of emergency water, some sandwiches and fruit. You should be okay for a day in here at least, but don't come out until I let you out, okay? I'm going to ask Papa for help."

The girl reached for Elisa's hand. She looked older than she had in the home spun. "Thank you."

CHAPTER TWENTY-THREE

"Elisa, you go. Take the grandchildren, go to your sister's. You take him,"—Giani hobbled from the door to the shop into the kitchen and pointed at Glen—"and send him for water." He handed a water carrier to Glen.

Giani grabbed the children's backpacks and shoved their drink bottles and random items from the table into them, and signalled for the children to move. He opened the back door. "Elisa, we have people coming. You go. You go now. He can come back with water. Show him where. You don't come back until I send for you, okay. Go. Go now."

Elisa looked over her shoulder at the safe room, but before she could say anything, her father grabbed her arm and pushed her toward the door.

"I no want you here at all, stay with Maria, you hear me? Glen, you tell me you trade water for something when you come back. Go, Elisa. Now."

The bell on the front door clanged as the door was shoved open. Giani pushed them out the door and locked it behind them.

"What the hell is going on, Glen?"

Glen picked up Elisa's niece and jogged ahead. Elisa was panting, trying to keep up. "There was trouble in the centre of town. A couple of Combers from down south lost something and asked the local Combers to help find it. Which is really weird. Anyway, one of the outsiders apparently found whatever it was, but clashed with police who had it, but it disappeared again. Several police were hurt by the southern bloke so they are back at your dad's, hoping to find the thing—whatever it is— and get this idiot out of town as fast as possible."

"Do we have any idea what this thing is?"

"Your dad does—he was reluctant to help them find it. What kind of things make your dad squeamish?"

Elisa stopped dead in her tracks. She looked back the way they had come and placed her palms on her cheeks. "Oh no."

It took a few steps for Glen to realise she had stopped. "What, Elisa? What's wrong?"

She turned tear-filled eyes to him. "People. The

only thing Papa refuses to find is people. Glen, there's a girl back there in the safe room. I found her in the alley. She's been treated so bad and I hid her. She was terrified of somebody finding her. She'd got handcuffs on. I think she might be the thing they lost. I feel sick. What if Papa puts them in the safe room with her?"

"Go to your sister's. Be safe, keep the kids safe. I'll help the girl, don't worry."

Reluctantly, Elisa took the children by the hands and jogged away. Glen turned back and ran to Giani's. He pounded on the door.

Giani pulled it open. "I no trade at my back door. You go to front where there is my shop," he yelled at Glen and waved his hands and arms around.

Understanding the message, Glen sprinted to the police station. He tried to recall the exact direction and felt time slow down. A few frustrating wrong turns had his heart beating rapidly, but finally he spotted it. He rushed through the doors, leaned over the polished counter, pulled in a huge breath and yelled. "The bloke you want is at Giani's."

He pivoted off the counter, turned and shoved open the doors, a cacophony of action behind him, pushed his feet into the ground, bunched his muscles and took off in an adrenaline-fuelled sprint back to Giani's swap shop.

The bell tinkled as he pushed open the door. Five men stood in the store—two were casually looking at the merchandise around them, and both appraised Glen as he entered. The other two were focussed on Giani.

Giani had his hands raised. "I don't know where this girl, this Cassie is."

"Cassie?" The name burst from Glen. The other men turned.

"You!" Harry bellowed and began to charge at him.

CHAPTER TWENTY-FOUR

The safe room was mostly dark, with cracks of light here and there to relieve the uniformity of shadowed space. From her foetal position on the makeshift bed, Cassie stared at the slivers of light, trying to make sense of how crazy her life had become.

She rolled onto her back and tears slid slowly down her cheeks into her hair.

What did I do to end up in this nightmare? I shouldn't cry, I haven't got enough water to waste it on tears.

The tears continued to slide. She wiped her eyes with the back of one hand, but the floodgates had opened and she rested both hands mid-brow, not trying to stem the flow. The metal of the cuffs tapped against her forehead as a very real reminder of the predicament she was in.

Water, water, everywhere but not a drop to drink. Dad used to say that all the time, I didn't know what it meant, but I loved him saying it. No one has enough water out here, how did it get to that?

She rolled onto her side, trying to find a comfortable way to avoid the worst of her bruises.

How did the country end up so wrecked? I was so wrong about everything. I didn't learn a thing at home. I have to get home. Will they take me back? Please let them take me back. I'll work my guts out if they just let me. They have to let me back.

Her whole body stiffened. Raised voices outside alerted her. She knew that voice.

No, no, no, no, he's found me? Did she betray me? How did he find me? If he finds me in here I'm dead.

She pushed herself hard into the corner of the room, trying to make herself as small as possible.

I've got to get out. No, she said to stay in here. No, I have to get away. I can't get out, he's in the way.

CHAPTER TWENTY-FIVE

The little bespectacled man urged the local Combers to stop Harry ploughing through Glen. They grabbed the bigger man and held him back. Glen figured they wouldn't be able to hold him long.

Giani, holding up a nasty looking mace, stepped over to Glen who was rapidly signing.

Glen brushed his index finger twice across his cheek—*girl*.

Giani pulled his brow down in a puzzled frown.

Glen pointed down with an index finger behind his other flat hand—*in*—and quickly followed by drawing a square in the air—*room*.

Giani's eyes widened, but there was no time for any other discussion, silent or otherwise.

"Where did you take her?" Harry bellowed. He pulled the other two forward, straining to reach Glen. "She belongs to my boss. I'm gonna smash you both."

The small man stepped forward, nervously glancing at Harry, but addressing Glen. "Do you know where Cassie is? It would seem logical for you to try and take back your salvage, and the coincidence of you being here just as she has left our company seems highly unlikely."

"Even if I did know where she was, I wouldn't tell you bastards. You treated her worse than your dogs. I'm here on trade business, but if I'd known you scum had her here I would have done something sooner."

"You know this girl?" Giani asked in a mix of shock and anger. "How she salvage? What—"

"Later, Giani, I'll explain later. Duck!"

Harry broke free of his restraint, shoving the others to the floor and launched himself at Glen and Giani, reaching with murderous hands for them. Both dived under the counter and ran for the back room. The counter was old, solid, and heavy, and would stop Harry for only a few moments.

They heard the destruction of it as they reached the kitchen.

Giani fumbled with the locks, but managed to get the door open as Harry lurched into the room, mere steps behind them.

Giani stumbled on the stairs and hobbled across the stones of the road. He stopped at the mouth of the alley and lifted the mace. "I'm old, Glen. I stay and defend."

Glen spun around and sprinted back, launching himself between Giani and the destructive mountain of Harry. The impact sent both Glen and Harry skidding across the path.

CHAPTER TWENTY-SIX

I can't sit in here like a victim. I have to face this. How the heck do I open this door?

The sense of purpose sliding through Cassie was probably adrenaline, but she didn't care.

This has got to stop. I may never get home, but I can't keep living in this cloud of fear. Nobody owns me except me.

Cassie found the lock mechanism and slid it open, carefully scanning the room to see if anyone was there. Moving as quietly as she could, she stepped into the kitchen. Two men stood in the alley outside the door.

At the other end of the alley, she could make out two men fighting. She recognised the bulk of Harry and the hair rose on her arms and neck. She felt cold but determined.

Quieter than before, so as not to alert the watchers in the alley, she moved towards the door opposite and slid down the passageway away from the danger. She climbed over a splintered countertop and pulled open the door.

The bell tinkled merrily and loud.

Specs stood in her way. "Cassie, you must come with me. I work for New Melbourne. They have transport waiting for you. I know you have no reason to trust me, but please, while Harry is distracted by Glen, we have a few minutes to get you on your way home. Come now, please."

"Glen? From Melton? Is that who Harry is beating up?"

"It doesn't matter. Come on, we haven't much time. They have been searching for you since you went missing. I tried to help you in Airport, but I can't blow my cover. Please, come now."

"It matters." Cassie stepped back into the shop and looked around for something hard and heavy. She grabbed a solid metal wedge-shaped tool with a handle and hefted it once or twice. "It matters to me." She stepped back onto the street, ignoring Specs, and walked quickly toward the alley. "Hairy."

The inarticulate roar told her he had heard her. She lifted the metal wedge above her head and waited.

"Hairy. I have a present for you."

He struggled to free himself from Glen's grip, but Glen held fast.

Without hesitation, she brought the heavy metal down on the back of Harry's thick neck. He grunted, fell and stopped moving. Cassie dropped the wedge onto the ground.

Glen looked up from under Harry.

Cassie stared at him. "I'll find a way to pay you back."

"You don't owe us anything, Cassie. It's we who owe you."

Cassie shrugged. "I'm going home."

Glen watched her walk away and shoved the unconscious Harry off him.

Giani sat panting on his doorstep.

"We'll take this mess with us, Giani. The sharks could do with a good feed."

The local Combers hooked their arms under Harry's and dragged him away.

Cassie turned the corner where Specs was waiting and indicated with her palm that he should lead the way. "You have somewhere to take me? Come on then."

Three minutes later the police arrived to an alley full of nothing.

EPILOGUE

"Breakfast, honey, come join us outside."

"Two minutes, Mum." Cassie checked her room for any last-minute items, making sure everything that stayed behind was well secured. She lifted her backpack and her suitcase and carried them into the living room.

"Morning, Dad." She walked into his embrace.

"Morning, pumpkin." He kissed the top of her head. "Are you set?"

"All set."

They climbed up to the deck and sat at the little wrought iron table for breakfast.

"We are so proud of you. You do know that? We've always been proud of you."

"I do now. Thanks for staying with me all this time.

It's been months and I know you had big jobs you left to be here, but I really needed you."

"We know, honey. What kind of teachers would we be if we couldn't leave the work to our students?" Her Mother patted Cassie's hand and smiled lovingly.

"What kind of parents would we be if we couldn't put our baby first occasionally?"

"Dad." Cassie rolled her eyes, then hugged her dad.

"I'm sorry, love, we thought we were doing what was best. The world needs help, we need to do what we can." He put his hands up in a placating gesture. "I know, I know, it isn't going anywhere today."

"No, but I am. Just a little less dramatically this time."

They all laughed.

"Eat up, you have a boat to catch. They are waiting for you."

Cassie enthusiastically bit into her favourite breakfast of seaweed roll.

***

The room was decorated with the diagrams Cassie had carefully drafted. The desks and chairs were a mixture of centuries and materials, but all of them were scrubbed clean and ready for the students. Cassie had traded credits with the Combers for them.

Cassie's stomach gurgled and her skin tingled with anticipation. She was breathing a little rapidly.

The door opened and she smiled in welcome.

The classroom filled swiftly.

Several familiar faces looked back at her. Elisa smiled and put up both thumbs.

"Hello, my name is Cassie Orm, and yes I am the daughter of *those* Orms. I grew up on New Melbourne and I love it there, but it took a rather uncomfortable journey of discovery to make me realise that what we had in my home was not available to everyone."

The sea of faces were fully focused, so eager to learn, and it warmed her heart.

"New Melbourne is trying to teach as many people to be engineers and scientists as it can comfortably train within the limits of its space and resources. They are the big picture people, the innovative dreamers and planners. We need more people like that. But here, I am going to teach you how to fix things. We need ten times as many fixers than dreamers. The only way we can make this country work is if we all know how to fix it. I am here today to help you discover how. Welcome to Djerriwah trade school."

The class applauded, and in the pocket of sound Cassie looked across at Glen.

Glen put his thumb up from his fist—*good*—and brushed his finger across his cheek twice—*girl*.

She frowned at him and made an okay sign that she moved toward him—*not*—and wiped her finger across her cheek twice—*girl*. Then she pointed to her chest—*I*—and moved a gun-shaped hand with the index finger pointed upward, back and forward—*teacher*.

He put two flat hands with thumbs up, palm to back and moved the hand closest toward her—*More*. Tilting a fist, he flicked up the thumb—*than*—and repeated her sign for *teacher*. He lifted both palms up and down—*Much*—and repeated his first sign—*more*. All of which only took thirty seconds.

Cassie began her class with a glowing smile.

ABOUT THE AUTHOR

C A Clark is a cross-genre writer of fantasy, SF, horror, dystopia, the odd bit of romance, children's stories and memoir. Creating stories is akin to breathing for C A Clark.

C A Clark has a growing body of short stories including eight with antipodeanSF at https://antisf.com/

C A Clark is a social media Luddite however this is changing.

ABOUT DEADSET PRESS

Deadset Press is the publishing imprint for Aussie Speculative Fiction – a community aimed at supporting Australian and Kiwi authors. You can learn more at:

www.aussiespeculativefiction.com

ABOUT THE SERIES

Drowned Earth is a series of eight standalone novellas, set in a shared world.

Prequel: Shards of Silver by Alanah Andrews

Debbie is on board a ship when an asteroid collides with Antarctica, causing a tsunami. And it's heading her way...
(eBook Only: Free Download)

The Rise by Sue-Ellen Pashley

The great Rise means that resources are scarce and not readily shared. But with her best friend's life at stake, along with some stranded refugees, Katie James knows she must prove there's more to being human than just existing. Even if that puts her on the same kill list.

Fire Over Troubled Water by Nick Marone

Despite winds, torrential rains, storms, and bushfires, a fresh water merchant searches for his lost daughter among the autonomous island communities of flooded eastern New South Wales.

Submerged City by Austin P. Sheehan

Melbourne is under martial law, overseen by general Messinger—an extremist who believes the flood is God's retribution against the left-wing agenda. . .

Tides of War by Marcus Turner

After discovering a strange man in a row boat, Maria wages war on the lotus cities—clandestine floating communities off the coast of Victoria that are reserved for the wealthy.

The Jindabyne Secret by Jo Hart

With nothing but a map and a rickety solar truck, Jax journeys to the top secret fresh water facility at Lake Jindabyne—one of the few fresh water lakes left in Australia. What he discovers there could be the key to saving his whole community, as long as the government doesn't kill him first.

River of Diamonds by S. M. Isaac

Who would want to leave one of the last idyllic settlements since the Rise? Rosa has a map, a mercenary, and a hope to salvage a future for the world.

Emoto's Promise by Shel Calopa

Five hundred years after the flood, can Macie defeat the technology which has enslaved the last remaining humans in the walled city of Darwin?

Salvaged by C.A. Clark

Cassie lives in the safe haven of academics on the anchored city of new Melbourne. After a diving incident she is rescued by a territorial beach combing gang who trade goods washed up by the frequent storms. Cassie wishes she had never taken her home for granted.

ALSO BY DEADSET PRESS

Annual Anthologies

Beginnings: Australian Speculative Fiction Vol. 1

Journeys: Australian Speculative Fiction Vol. 2

Zodiac Series

Capricorn

Aquarius

Pisces

www.aussiespeculativefiction.com